The terrorist army cheered wildly

Rafael Encizo had been felled by a swift lashing kick to his head. His opponent—his long-lost brother Raul—approached and raised his booted foot to stomp the breath out of him. Rafael swiftly rolled out of reach, then paused and looked up through the blood slowly dripping into his eyes.

"I don't blame you for any of this, Raul. It's not your fault—you've been brainwashed by Castro's Cuba."

A look of denial, of fury, swept across Raul's face. The crowd held its breath in anticipation as he shouted a karate *kiai* and charged at Rafael in an all-out determination to wipe out the words and their source.

Mack Bolan's
PHOENIX FORCE.

PHOENIX FORCE.

GAR WILSON

JUNGLE SWEEP

A GOLD EAGLE BOOK FROM
WORLDWIDE.

TORONTO • NEW YORK • LONDON • PARIS
AMSTERDAM • STOCKHOLM • HAMBURG
ATHENS • MILAN • TOKYO • SYDNEY

First edition January 1989

ISBN 0-373-61339-3

Special thanks and acknowledgment to
William Fieldhouse for his contribution to this work.

Printed in U.S.A.

1

If the past reflects the future, historians ought to be the best fortune-tellers, Robert Newton thought as he swatted a mosquito at the back of his neck. The insect had already pierced his skin and sucked in enough blood to become a crimson smear on his palm. He glanced at it, aware that it was his own blood. The insects had already gotten a lot of his blood over the past three days, and Newton figured he would be anemic before they returned to Mexico City.

Seeing himself panting and sweating in a tropical jungle in southern Mexico was one thing he hadn't included in his plans. A high school history teacher from Chaska, Minnesota, Newton had wanted to do something different during his summer vacation months. He had saved as much money as possible—no easy task on the meager salary of a schoolteacher—for his big adventure in Mexico. Divorced for more than a year, he had been looking forward to his first big vacation as a swinging bachelor far from the eyes and ears of the Chaska Board of Education. Being a walking blood-mobile for thousands of hungry mosquitoes had not been part of his plans for a big holiday.

But then Newton had not expected to meet Gerald Harrimon, either. Harrimon was an ambitious young archaeologist from Boston, a rather dashing man who resembled a young John Kennedy and possessed the persuasive powers of a natural-born politician. Newton met Harrimon at the National Museum of Anthropology. The two North Americans were pleased to encounter each other. They were fellow countrymen in a foreign land and shared common interests in Mexican history and pre-Columbian culture.

That had led to a discussion of the artifacts on display in the museum and the archaeological wonders of the Mayan and Aztec civilizations. Newton had always been fascinated by the remarkable accomplishments of these ancient people, the great Indian civilizations that had ruled Mexico and most of Central America before the arrival of Cortez and the Spanish conquistadores.

Harrimon was quite knowledgeable of the Mayan ruins of Mexico and northern Guatemala. He had told Newton about a recent visit to the excavations at El Mirador. Harrimon claimed it had been one of the oldest and largest of the ancient Mayan cities. He described the Tigre Temple in detail and related that bits of pottery helped to date the site as more than two thousands years old.

The archaeologist also claimed there was evidence of another Mayan ruin in southern Mexico near the base of the Yucatán peninsula and the Guatemalan border. Harrimon explained that he hoped to hire a guide and get necessary supplies for his quest, but after exhausting all his funding, including personal moneys, he was still short by a certain sum, not huge but enough to keep him from the go-ahead. Newton decided it was a once-in-a-lifetime opportunity to be part of a thrilling new archaeological discovery and offered to give Harrimon the money if he could join the exploration team.

The idea had made a lot more sense in Mexico City than it did after three and a half days of trekking through the Yucatán jungle. The guide had turned out to be an alcoholic liar who had only a vague familiarity with the area. The stoop-backed, toothless con artist had said his name was Ramon, but Newton suspected the name was a lie, as well.

Still, the fellow knew the Yucatán better than Harrimon. The confident young archaeologist had never attempted an expedition on his own before, and the task proved more difficult than he had anticipated. Newton figured Harrimon was eager for the fame and recognition of making a great new discovery of Mayan artifacts. Probably he daydreamed about selling articles to *National Geographic* and maybe a TV special, and Newton had to admit such notions had also played a part in motivating him.

Newton had thought it would be great to return to Chaska and tell everybody how he spent his summer vacation uncovering secrets of history instead of simply reading about them. His students would surely take a different view of him then. To break the monotonous cycle of his life seemed worth a bit of risk.

Ramon got them lost twice. With the aid of his compass, Harrimon managed to get them back on track. By the third day Newton was getting worried. After all, how much could Harrimon really know about the alleged Mayan site if he had such vague ideas about where it was located?

Newton also had trouble with the physical demands of the journey. Most of his thirty-seven years had been spent behind a desk, and he was not in peak physical condition. At least he was glad he had quit smoking several years ago because the spare tire around his middle and the generally flabby condition of his muscles was enough of a strain without a poor oxygen supply, as well.

Harrimon was about ten years younger than Newton and in much better shape. The young archaeologist had little trouble hacking through the vines and monster ferns blocking their path. The jungle was very green and thickly walled by tall grass, oversize plants and trees draped with vines, and the gnarled and raised roots seemed to always present some sort of problem for the three-man team.

Ramon tended to ramble on and on about life in general and himself in particular. He claimed he had once been a successful merchant and salesman, a vital link for businesses in both Mexico and the United States. Newton had no idea if any of the stories were true. Ramon guzzled so much tequila his words were frequently slurred and jumbled. But he was their only guide, and when sober he seemed to know what he was doing. Unfortunately he wasn't sober very often.

Newton was just about ready to tell the others that he quit, and rather than go any farther he would demand they go back to Mexico City. He was soaked with sweat. His khaki shirt smelled and stuck to his wet armpits and his shorts were plastered to his rump. At that moment he wished he had never left his air-conditioned hotel room, but even more, that he had never ventured from the cool clean state of Minnesota.

He was jolted out of his glum mood unexpectedly.

"We found it!" Harrimon exclaimed, and began hacking away a curtain of thick branches from a pair of gum trees. "I told you we'd find it!"

"Si, si," Ramon said, bobbing his head. "Was there any doubt, *señor*?"

Newton rushed forward and nearly ran into Harrimon's flashing machete. The young archaeologist was swinging the big jungle knife with frenzied zeal, all his calm, collected appearance gone as he eagerly chopped through the barricade of foliage between himself and the discovery. Newton was nearly as excited as Harrimon, but he forced himself to stand back. It was safer than stepping within range of the archaeologist's machete. Besides, it was Harrimon's moment of glory. Newton realized that his role in the discovery came second. Still, there would be enough recognition to go around.

The Minnesota teacher was chiding himself for being faint of heart and for wishing he had never come to Mexico let alone wanting to join Harrimon on the expedition. He was already thinking of possible titles for *National Geographic* features as he fumbled with his Minolta camera. He eagerly waited for Harrimon to clear away the brush so he could see the wonderful discovery for himself.

"Oh, God," Harrimon gasped. "This is so great."

"This is it?" Newton replied lamely.

He had expected to see the crumbled steps to a temple ruin or perhaps an ancient Mayan pyramid-like structure. All Harrimon had found was a pile of rocks at the base of a boulder. Newton shook his head with disappointment. He felt cheated. Instead of finding a hidden city of a lost civilization, they had stumbled upon some oversize pebbles.

"I knew we would find it, *señor*," Ramon repeated. He glanced down at the pile of stones, shrugged and took a bottle of tequila from his pants pocket.

Harrimon knelt by the rubble and began examining the stones as if he had found a diamond mine. Newton wondered if the guy had cracked up. Maybe it was heatstroke, he thought, or a delusion caused by the difficult trek in the oppressive heat and humidity coupled with the desperate hope of coming across an incredible archaeological treasure. Harrimon was probably so anxious about making a great find that he had convinced himself that a bunch of rocks was a Mayan marvel.

"Look at this, Robert," Harrimon remarked enthusiastically as he handed Newton a thin, slightly curved piece of stone.

"Yeah," the teacher responded, but there was no elation in his voice. He took the stone, then blinked with surprise. It was not a stone. Harrimon had handed him a broken piece of pottery. It appeared to be some sort of earthenware with a faded red line along the surface.

"Is this Mayan?" Newton asked. "Are you positive?"

"Absolutely," Harrimon replied. "Chicanelware. Very similar to that found by the ruins of the east gate of the Sacred Wall in El Mirador."

"I'll be damned," Newton whispered. He looked down at the collection of stones at the base of the boulder with new interest. "What else is there?"

"You see this?" Harrimon began, giving him a small, thick stone object resembling white marble.

Newton examined it. The stone was smooth and had probably been well polished. One end was curved, rather like a bird's beak, and the other had a semicircle carved into stone. It looked vaguely familiar to the history teacher.

"Any idea what that is?" Harrimon asked.

"It sort of reminds me of one of the hieroglyph figures of the Mayan calendar," Newton replied.

"Good guess," Harrimon told him. "But it is actually a piece of a ceremonial mask used in a ritual to the god Kukulcan."

"Kukulcan?" Newton strained his memory. "Wasn't that the Mayan god of creation? Usually depicted as a feathered serpent like Quetzalcoatl in Aztec mythology?"

"Right," Harrimon confirmed. "The Aztecs probably ripped off Kukulcan and turned him into Quetzalcoatl the same way the Romans took the Greek gods like Zeus and Poseidon and renamed them Jupiter and Neptune."

"Fascinating," Newton said, staring down at the collection of relics that he had formerly regarded as rock rubble.

"Gringos," Ramon muttered as he sucked on his bottle. *"Muy loco."*

Among the rubble Newton noticed a small object that resembled tarnished metal, and bending over, he picked up what seemed to be a two-inch tube of copper. He knitted his eyebrows and frowned. Although he did not know much about firearms and ammunition, even he could identify the copper object as the shell casing from a rifle cartridge.

"What the hell?" Harrimon began, staring at the casing. "How did that get here?"

The roar of an automatic rifle erupted from the jungle. Ramon fell backward against the trunk of a gum tree. Ragged bullet holes had cut a diagonal line across his chest. The tequila bottle slipped from his trembling fingers and shattered near his feet. Ramon slumped to the ground at the base of the tree. Blood spilled from his open mouth as his head drooped forward. Then he twitched slightly for the last time and fell sideways lifelessly.

"Jesus Christ!" Harrimon exclaimed as he jumped to his feet.

Newton threw himself to the ground. His heart raced and his body trembled with fear as he clung to the earth. Unfamiliar with combat, he dove to the ground because he vaguely recalled reading or hearing that one is supposed to do that when there is any shooting. Horrified, he did not want to look at Ramon's body so he glanced about in every other direction.

He saw the ferns and grass part as legs clad in jungle camouflage trousers marched forward. Booted feet trampled the ground and rifle barrels pushed aside low-hanging branches. Newton shook so badly he feared his bones would shatter. The men who had appeared from the jungle seemed to be soldiers of some sort. Why had they opened fire? Newton's numb mind asked, but for an answer he only had a dreadful premonition that they would be killed for sure.

"No!" Harrimon cried. "Please don't! *Por favor...*"

The archaeologist had tried to run from the mysterious gunmen but discovered that he was surrounded by armed opponents. Newton saw Harrimon raise his arms and walk backward. Several soldiers had blocked Harrimon's escape route. Newton saw their rifles pointed at the archaeologist. He saw the hard faces of the gunmen, dark and unshaven, their eyes narrowed, yet the orbs gleaming with blood lust.

One of them smiled and triggered his weapon. Flame burst from the muzzle, and the sound of the assault rifle hammered Newton's ears like invisible fists. Harrimon's body jerked from the force of the hits, then Newton saw the exit wounds as the bullets burst from Harrimon's back. They had punched clean through him. Blood oozed from the awful holes as Gerald Harrimon staggered backward. His body wilted to the ground.

"Oh, God," Newton whispered as he closed his eyes and began to pray. He had not prayed much since he had grown up, but he discovered it came very naturally under the circumstances.

The sound of advancing footsteps told Newton someone was getting closer. He kept his eyes closed, fearful of looking up to see death waiting to claim him. Newton lay on his belly, facedown and arms outstretched with his fingers interlaced in prayer.

A boot heel smashed down on his hands, making bones pop. Newton groaned from the pain. The punishing boot ground the crushed fingers into the earth. Agony burned along the nerves, and Newton tried to pull his hands free. His tormentor laughed at his plight and again stomped on Newton's broken fingers.

The schoolteacher cried out and rolled away from the sadist, his hands trembling and useless, the fingers bent and twisted. Bone splinters poked through the skin at the second knuckle of his right index finger. Next a hard kick to his stomach knocked the breath from his lungs, and his body jackknifed in an attempt to find some protection.

One of the soldiers decided to join his comrade in the cruel game. He stepped forward and kicked Newton in the left kidney. The teacher groaned and tried to crawl away, still afraid to open his eyes, but a boot heel stamped down on the nape of his neck and another stomped him at the small of the back.

A kick to the ribs made him flop over onto his back. One of the tormentors stomped a heel into the center of Newton's chest, and the sternum cracked. The side of his head received a vicious blow and another was aimed at his face. He was already unconscious before another kick broke his jawbone and dislodged two teeth.

The soldiers still went at it, smashing bones and driving splintered shards into Newton's heart and lungs. A giggling brute stomped a boot into the bridge of Newton's nose. Blood squirted from his eyes like scarlet tears as orbital bone cracked. The sight pleased the assailants, but Robert Newton was beyond caring. They had already killed him.

"¡*Basta!*" a voice bellowed. "Enough! The man is dead. They are all dead."

"*Si, Capitán,*" the tall, muscle-bound brute who had started the beating said with a smile. "They are all dead. We took care of them with no trouble, eh?"

The captain shook his head. He was slightly shorter than the other men and not as heavily muscled, yet his physique was sculptured like a professional athlete's. His ruggedly handsome face was marred by a birthmark under his right eye. He glanced down at the three corpses and sighed.

"Don't be too proud of your victory, Garcia," he told the larger man. "None of the men you killed were armed. None of them were fighters."

"They are *gringos*," Garcia insisted, puffing out his barrel chest. The buttons of his uniform shirt strained until they nearly popped. "They may be CIA spies or NSA."

"Not very likely,"the captain replied. "No matter. The *norteamericanos* are our enemies regardless of what profession they might have."

"Si." Garcia smiled. "Anyway, they were getting too close to our base. Major Pescador left strict orders—"

"I am aware of those orders," the captain told him. "I am not criticizing you, but I am warning all of you to realize this encounter is barely a training exercise."

He walked to Ramon's body and pointed at the broken bottle beside it. "This one was just an old drunkard," the captain declared. "A *mejicano* bootlicker who prostituted himself for *yanqui* dollars. The other two were probably tourists who came here looking for adventure. None of them could fight back. Other opponents in the future will not be so easy."

"I welcome the challenge," Garcia said, and gestured toward his comrades. "We all do."

"Then you'd better be ready for it when the time comes," the captain replied. "Get rid of the bodies and meet me back at the base."

2

Rafael Encizo arrived at the San Diego airport in late afternoon. Dressed in a light blue business suit with a blue-and-white striped shirt and a maroon necktie, he appeared to be an executive on a business trip or a corporate salesman planning to peddle some venture to a firm in southern California.

Although he could and often did look dangerous, Encizo was a ruggedly attractive man who had been compared to a number of movie and television stars of Hispanic or Italian heritage. His dark good looks and athletic physique, combined with a natural charm and pleasant manner, appealed to men and women alike and made them feel at ease with Encizo. He appeared to be at least ten years younger than his true age and his straight posture and confident stride gave the impression he was taller than five foot ten.

An observant eye might have noticed a small white strip of scar tissue above Encizo's left temple or a curious circular scar in the palm of his right hand. One would probably assume these were remnants of some nasty accident, perhaps from a car crash or an industrial mishap. Actually, the marks were all mementos of his past.

The Cuban-born adventurer had survived a thousand close encounters with violent death and had thus far cheated the Grim Reaper every time. His career had started nearly three decades ago as a boy in Cuba during the communist revolution. His parents had been murdered by the political purge that followed Castro's takeover. His younger brother and sisters had been taken away by the soldiers and his older brother was killed. Only Rafael managed to flee to the mountains to join a band of guerrillas.

But the effort was doomed to failure against Castro's seasoned troops, and it was lucky that young Rafael and a handful of survivors managed to escape to the United States.

Encizo returned to Cuba with the Bay of Pigs invasion and wound up as a political prisoner in El Principe, from where he eventually had managed to escape after enduring near starvation, beatings and torture. He returned to the United States and decided to pick up the pieces of his life.

He became a naturalized U.S. citizen and before finding his true calling, worked in a number of different professions that ranged from being a scuba instructor to doing jobs for the Drug Enforcement Agency, Justice Department and the FBI.

Encizo was employed as an insurance investigator specializing in maritime claims when he was contacted by a covert government agency and asked to join a new top-secret enforcement outfit known as Stony Man Operations. He had been one of five men chosen for a commando unit called Phoenix Force.

A unique team of the best professionals trained in counter-terrorism, covert operations and virtually every form of combat, Phoenix Force was established to take on missions that the CIA, NSA and other intelligence or military units were unable to deal with. Phoenix Force was predominantly a means of fighting international terrorism. Increasingly, modern-day barbarians threatened the interests of the United States and other democracies, and frequently directly endangered the lives of American citizens.

Encizo had received most of his scars since joining up with Phoenix Force. The missions had been incredibly high-risk operations, and the men consistently faced enormous odds in battling dangerous opponents, among them terrorists of every type, criminal syndicates and enemy espionage networks.

However his reason for being in San Diego did not concern Phoenix Force. He was on a personal mission of sorts, yet it was potentially as dangerous as anything he had participated in during his long career as a warrior and adventurer.

MANUEL CASSIAS WAITED for Encizo to arrive on Flight 507 from Washington, D.C. A short, round man in baggy tan slacks and a brown sport jacket, Cassias was the sort of man one barely granted a second glance. His plump cheeks were always covered with a smattering of black stubble and his shoulder-length hair was generally uncombed and tangled-looking, like a black mop head. The man's wide grin made casual observers wonder if he was simpleminded.

Cassias may have looked like a buffoon, but that appearance was deceptive. Encizo had known him for more than a decade and appreciated Cassias's intelligence, cunning and skill. A Mexican-American who generally operated out of El Paso, Texas, Cassias was a top-notch smuggler. He would not handle drugs or guns but was ready to deal in just about anything else. He smuggled American cigarettes and whiskey into Mexico and sneaked liqueurs and craft goods from Mexico into the U.S. Among his assortment of merchandise people were occasionally found as cargo to be surreptitiously transported from Mexico into the United States or vice versa.

Although technically a criminal, Cassias did not do business with drug dealers, white slavers, murderers or political extremists. However he was privy to a fair amount of information about underworld activities, and in the past he had shared some of this knowledge with Encizo. They had done each other several favors over the years, but Cassias still owed Encizo a big one, dating from the time Rafael Encizo had saved Cassias's life when the smuggler had run afoul of a gang of Colombian syndicate hoods.

"Rafael," Cassias greeted as he embraced the Cuban like a brother. "It has been a long time, my friend. Almost ten years, no?"

"A very long time," Encizo confirmed. "Let's get my luggage and leave so we can talk in private."

"Of course," Cassias agreed. "Are you using your own name these days?"

"Hardly ever," Encizo replied. "I'm using an easy one this time. Rafael Emmanuel Sanchez."

"I think I can remember that," Cassias said as they headed for the baggage claim section. "We'd better hurry. I arranged the meeting for tonight."

"Good," Encizo said with a nod. "I was afraid we wouldn't be able to touch base with Alverez for a few days."

"He sees it as an easy way to make ten thousand dollars," Cassias said with a shrug. "That's a lot of money just for a photograph."

"It's worth it to me," Encizo told him.

They collected Encizo's luggage at the baggage claim section. The Cuban carried his suitcase and garment bag as he followed Cassias into the parking lot. They put his baggage in the trunk of a battered old Ford sedan, then Cassias slid behind the wheel and Encizo sat next to him.

"I wasn't able to come up with much as far as guns are concerned," Cassias stated. "Two .38 snubnose revolvers, a .357 Magnum and a Marlin .30-30."

"I don't plan to shoot Alverez," Encizo stated. "I'm prepared to make a straight deal with him."

"That's nice, Rafael," Cassias remarked as he started the engine. "But don't forget Alverez isn't a nice man. He's a member of the Mexican mafia. Don't forget he's a killer. He'll probably have some of his *amigos* along. They're killers, too."

"Yeah," Encizo replied. "I've met killers before."

"I know," Cassias acknowledged with a nod as he backed the Ford out of the parking space.

Cassias knew that Encizo was a brave man and that he was the best fighting man Cassias had ever met. But he also remembered the terrible nightmare in Galveston when the Colombians had him strapped to a chair as they tortured him for information.

It seemed as though he could smell his own burned flesh again and feel the razor's sharp slivers of pain as the memories of that night in Galveston flooded into Manuel Cassias's mind and filled him with uneasiness about the current prospect. Manuel thought it strange to have such foreboding thoughts even though they were driving along Seaport Village, a pleasant and colorful section of San Diego located along the piers. Ships and pleasure craft sailed in the blue water of the bay beneath a clear and sunny California sky. Cassias had always favored San Diego over Los Angeles. The pace was slower, the city less crowded, and the people tended to be more polite and considerate. San Diego had the nickname "America's Finest City" and, although Cassias called El Paso home, he was inclined to agree with the nickname.

Maybe he would retire to San Diego. If he lived to retire, that is, he thought. Two more years of smuggling and wheeling-dealing and he ought to have a large enough nest egg to give up his shady business. He noticed a reproduction of a pirate ship docked in the harbor. It would be nice to spend a day on the decks of that exotic vessel, Cassias mused as he drove past the wooden hull and great white sail with the Jolly Roger banner flying from the mast. It would be pleasant to take a cruise on the ship and enjoy a superb seafood dinner in one of the fine restaurants in Seaport Village afterward.

A nice daydream, and maybe he would do these things at some later date. He mused that he would not be alive to contemplate future pleasures if Rafael Encizo had not put his own life on the line to save Cassias's. The Cuban had rescued him from a horror of agony and torture that would have made death as welcome as a glass of iced tea on a summer day.

Whenever Encizo asked him for a favor, Cassias immediately responded. He owed the Cuban a debt he could never truly repay. Whatever Encizo wanted, Cassias was prepared to do, even at the cost of his own life, if necessary.

"Where does Alverez want to meet with me?" Encizo asked, drawing Cassias back from his memories and daydreams.

"At a warehouse near San Ysidro," Cassias replied. "That's right by the border. Most of the country probably still associates it with that shooting spree at a McDonald's restaurant. A guy named James Huberty went nuts and killed twenty-one people a few years ago."

"That was one incident, and it was quite some time ago," Encizo said. "What's the place like most of the time?"

"Most of the citizens are law-abiding," Cassias answered, steering the Ford into the right-hand lane. "Mostly Hispanic, lower middle-class, and many businesses there are influenced by their location at the border. A lot of money-exchange operations— some illegal. There's also some gang violence and occasional problems from *coyotes*. I'm not talking about the four-legged kind."

Encizo knew what he meant. A *coyote* could be a shyster lawyer, an expression used mostly in Mexico, but the *coyotes* Cassias referred to were crooked "travel agents" involved in smuggling illegal immigrants across the border. *Coyotes* were not humanitarians. They would help the immigrants across the border for a price—generally everything they had. Often they would simply lead the would-be immigrants to a remote area and kill them for whatever they may have had stashed away on their bodies.

The *coyotes* also clashed with the Border Patrol from time to time. Modern-day *bandidos*, they were not frightened by the patrols and would not hesitate to exchange gunfire with the border cops. The Border Patrol had been said to have the most dangerous beat in the United States.

"Alverez wants to meet with you alone," Cassias continued. "Be careful with that one. He'd sell his own mother into white slavery if he thought he could make ten dollars in the deal. He won't bat an eyelash if he figures killing you will be the easiest way to get what he wants."

"I've met the type before," Encizo assured him. "When does he want to meet me?"

"Nine o'clock tonight," Cassias answered, "at an abandoned warehouse." Encizo grunted. "And it's in an area where gunshots aren't especially unusual. I guess Alverez wants to be in a place where disturbances will probably be ignored by most of the population." Cassias paused, then said grimly, "Maybe you should forget this, Rafael."

"I really can't," Encizo replied. "It's one of those things I can't turn my back on. It's personal, Manuel."

"That's what I was afraid you'd say," Cassias muttered with a sigh.

ENCIZO DROVE THE FORD to the row of warehouses at the outskirts of San Ysidro. The gates to the steel-wire fence stood open, and Encizo simply drove inside the compound. No security guard was stationed at the storage buildings, but lights were on in only one warehouse. The Cuban glanced at his wristwatch. It was 2050 hours. He was ten minutes early.

He parked the sedan and switched off the lights and the engine. A familiar cold ball of fear formed in the pit of his stomach. Anyone sitting in a car in a dark, remote area awaiting a clandestine meeting with a gangster would likely experience apprehension. Only a fool would feel confident in such a situation.

Encizo realized he was exposing himself to certain unavoidable risks. Alverez and his men might simply shoot him as he sat in the car, although that possibility didn't seem too real because they would suspect he would not be carrying all his money to the meeting. The agreement was to bring five thousand cash and have the rest available after the deal was complete. Still, there was no way of being sure what a small-time mobster like Alverez might do.

Two figures approached the car, and Encizo waited patiently for the pair to draw near. Seeing them closer, he came to the conclusion that they could have served as human bookends. Both young-ish-looking men were large, had long black hair, clipped beards, and stony eyes that dominated their hard faces. They wore dark blue shirts and slacks with brown loafers, and because they looked almost like twins, the easiest way to tell them apart seemed to be by their weapons. One held a cut-down pump shotgun, and the other carried a stainless-steel revolver with a six-inch barrel.

Moonlight bathed the pair, and Encizo clearly saw the muzzle of the shotgun pointed at the windshield of the Ford. He was tempted to duck under the dash and draw the .38 snubnose Smith & Wesson from his belt. His battle-honed instincts wanted to respond immediately, roar into action and stomp on the gas pedal, duck and run the joker over. To stay seated behind the steering wheel and wait while the gun-men came closer was not easy.

"Get outta the car, man!" the pistolman ordered. His accent was more East L.A. than Sonora or Chi-huahua.

"Take it easy," Encizo replied as he slowly eased open the car door and slid outside, his hands held high.

"Spread-eagle, fella," the guy with the revolver ordered as he carefully came up to Encizo.

"There's a gun in my belt," Encizo admitted as he placed his hands on the roof of the car and spread his legs.

"Oh, yeah?" the hood snorted. He jammed the barrel of his revolver into the small of Encizo's back as his other hand slithered around the Cuban's waist to pluck the .38 from his belt. "How come you brought a piece?"

"Force of habit," Encizo replied.

The shotgun man kept his pump 12-gauge pointed at Encizo while the other hood frisked him. It was a rapid pat-down search. The man felt under Encizo's arms, the small of his back and down his legs to the ankles. He found Encizo's necktie in a jacket pocket.

"Planning to strangle somebody with this?" the hood snickered.

"I took it off to try to be comfortable," the Cuban answered, flicking the edge of his shirt collar open at the throat. "Not helping much now. You two don't need to point those cannons at me. I don't intend to put up a fight. I came to talk with Alverez. He's got something to sell and I came to buy it."

"Yeah," the hood said with a grin as he reached inside Encizo's jacket to remove a fat brown envelope from a pocket. "And here's the money, eh?"

"That's part of it," Encizo answered. "If you're thinking of killing me and taking the money and then lying to Alverez about it, better think again. I doubt if he'd take kindly to you trying to cheat him."

"Shut up," the thug hissed, jabbing Encizo in the ribs with his revolver. "Get your ass movin'. We're taking you to Mr. Alverez. Okay?"

"I'm thrilled about it," Encizo assured him. "Let's go."

The two gunmen escorted Encizo to the warehouse with lights in the window. The guy with the revolver walked in front of Encizo while the shotgun man followed behind. The door to the front office stood open, and they ushered him into a drab little room with a single window with the curtains drawn. Seated behind a desk was a man who appeared to be about forty years old. His wavy black hair had been professionally styled, and his fingernails were clean and manicured. He wore a white polo shirt with a little green alligator on the left breast. A gold Rolex watch with an eelskin band was strapped to his right wrist. The fingers of his left hand drummed the desk top near the ivory grips of a fancy Walther P-38 with a lot of gold inlays.

"Buenas noches," the hotshot behind the desk announced. "My friends don't speak English so well, so we speak English. Okay?"

"Either language is fine with me," Encizo replied with a nod. "You're Mr. Alverez?"

"That's right," the gangster replied, nodding his sleek head. "I don't exactly have a name for you."

"Maybe you should call him 'fathead,' Mr. Alverez," the hood with the revolver snorted as he placed Encizo's .38 on the desk. "I found this on him."

"Maybe I should call you 'fathead,' instead," Alverez snapped. "You're not with your asshole buddies in the barrio. You show some respect. Don't talk unless I tell you to. Understand?"

"Yes, sir," the hood answered glumly.

Alverez looked at the snubnose revolver with disinterest. He would have been more suspicious if their guest had not come armed. After all, the *hombre* knew that Alverez was with the Mexican mafia. He did not give a damn about the gun. All he wanted to know about was the money.

"As I was saying before I was interrupted," Alverez began, aiming a sneer at his humiliated henchman. "What's your name?"

"My driver's license says I'm named Sanchez," Encizo answered with a shrug. "Does it matter?"

"Not if I get my money," Alverez answered. "Did you bring it?"

"Fathead took it," the Cuban replied.

The henchman glared at Encizo. The other hood, the shotgun man, snickered at his partner's embarrassment. Alverez snapped his fingers. Fathead took the envelope from his pocket and handed it to his boss. Alverez tore the envelope open and dumped out a bundle of hundred-dollar bills. He counted the money.

"Five thousand." He sighed. "It's in large bills. I didn't want anything bigger than a twenty."

"I got the money out of my personal savings account," Encizo explained. "There wasn't time to get it all broken into small bills."

"Where's the rest of the money?" Alverez asked.

"Show me the photographs and I'll tell you," the Cuban answered.

"Don't get smart, asshole," Fathead hissed.

"I don't think your boss told you to talk," Encizo commented. "Mr. Alverez has five thousand dollars in his hands. I haven't seen the photos. That's a big enough down payment for a product without seeing it."

"Fair enough," Alverez agreed as he opened a desk drawer and removed a manila envelope. "Take a look."

He handed it to Encizo. The Cuban removed three 8x10 photographs from the envelope. Several figures in camouflage fatigues stood among jungle ferns and tall grass. They were armed with Kalashnikov assault rifles. One of the soldiers was a muscular man with a strawberry-colored birthmark on his face.

"Where were these photos taken?" Encizo asked.

"Where's my money?" Alverez insisted.

Encizo took a key from his pocket and placed it on the desk. "There's a number on that key," he explained. "You'll find it fits a locker at the airport. Public lockers. No problem getting to them. The other five thousand is in a small, flat valise. You'll be happy to know the money is in small bills. Fives and tens.''

"Nice." Alverez smiled wolfishly. "What makes these photos so important to you, Sanchez?"

"Personal reasons," Encizo replied. "Now, will you please tell me what you know about these photos?"

"I know they're worth ten thousand dollars," Alverez commented. "Now, I think maybe they're worth more. Say, twenty thousand?"

"You have another buyer?" Encizo asked with a thin smile. "If not, you'd do well to stick with our original agreement."

"Ten thousand dollars is all I'll get, eh?" Alverez said with a sigh. "I guess we don't have anything left to discuss."

"Just tell me where the photos were taken," Encizo insisted.

"Kill him outside," Alverez instructed, putting a briefcase on his desk. "No reason to make a mess in here."

"It'll be a pleasure," Fathead announced, pointing his revolver at Encizo's face. "Let's go outside, and you can say goodbye to the world."

"Nice doing business with you, Sanchez," Alverez remarked as he began packing the money, the key, Encizo's .38 and his own P-38 into his briefcase. "Oh, I'll take the pictures. You won't need them and I may find another buyer. I found you, didn't I?''

Fathead snatched the pictures from Encizo's hand and gave them to Alverez. The shotgun man covered Encizo. The Cuban raised his hands to shoulder level and did not attempt to resist. Alverez stuck the photos in his briefcase and closed the lid.

"Who took the pictures?" Encizo asked once more.

"Fuck you," Fathead snorted. He waved his gun in the direction of the door. "Outside, asshole."

The shotgun man opened the door. The crack of a .30-30 rifle erupted outside, and the hoodlum dropped his shotgun and staggered backward, hands groping at the bullet hole in his chest. Blood spat from the quarter-size exit wound under his left shoulder blade. His heart stopped forever, and the man dropped to the floor.

Encizo immediately took advantage of the distraction. His right hand slapped Fathead's gunhand downward while with his left he quickly grabbed the wrist above the thug's revolver. The man pulled the trigger. His scream joined the roar of the big .44 Magnum as the powerful 200-grain hollowpoint bullet drilled through his right instep. The lead projectile expanded on impact to wreck several small bones in his foot. Blood seeped from the sole of his brown loafer.

The Cuban Phoenix Force pro held the wounded man's wrist with his left hand to keep the gun pointed at the floor. His right hand rose, and he bent his elbow to slam it under Fathead's jawbone. The thug's head bounced back from the blow, and Encizo's arm continued to rise. His right hand reached to the back of his collar and grabbed the hilt of the Gerber Mark 1 fighting knife in a sheath at the nape of his neck.

He had concealed the knife in that manner because it was a hiding place often missed by a casual frisk, especially when one willingly surrenders a weapon and calmly submits to a search. Encizo drew the dagger and swung the double-edged blade in a fast stroke across his opponent's neck. Blood jetted from the severed carotid artery. The cut had also sliced through the jugular and slit the Adam's apple. Fathead's weapon fell to the floor as he staggered backward into a wall. The thug slumped into a sitting position, his shirt drenched in crimson.

"¡Cristo!" Alverez exclaimed as he hastily wrenched open his briefcase in a desperate effort to grab one of the pistols stored there.

"Forget it, Alverez!" came a stern warning as Manuel Cassias appeared at the doorway, his Marlin .30-30 aimed at the mobster. "Try it and I'll kill you."

Alverez raised his hands in surrender. Encizo stepped forward, careful not to move between Cassias's rifle and Alverez. He scooped up the briefcase and closed the lid. The Cuban sat on the edge of the desk and pointed the tip of his bloodstained blade at Alverez. The Mexican gangster swallowed hard and nearly gagged on his fear.

"You're a very bad business man, Alverez," Encizo announced. "The deal we had was more than fair. You could have made ten thousand dollars for a few photographs you didn't need in the first place and a little information."

"So I made a mistake, okay?" Alverez began nervously. "We can make another deal...."

"I didn't like the idea of giving scum like you ten thousand dollars to begin with," Encizo told him. "The photographs are so important to me that I agreed to do business with you although I despise everything you are and everything you stand for. But now no more deals. You either tell me where the photos were taken and who took them, or I'll make you talk with this."

He gestured with the Gerber knife in his fist. Alverez squirmed in his chair, then glanced at Cassias. The smuggler was busy gathering up the weapons of the dead thugs. Alverez considered trying to jump Encizo while the Cuban was only armed with a knife, but wisely he decided not to try it after remembering the man's effectiveness with it.

"The pictures were taken in Mexico," Alverez declared. "Somewhere in the jungle region of the

Yucatán. I don't know where exactly. I swear to the Blessed Virgin that's the truth.''

"Now you're religious, huh?" Encizo snorted. "Who took the pictures?"

"One of my men down in Mexico," Alverez answered. "He got killed in a gunfight with some DEA agents last month. The photos were among his possessions when we went through his crib to see if he had anything else that could incriminate me or anybody else in my gang. That's when I found the pictures. I remembered hearing that some dude with connections with various Hispanic outfits had been trying to get a lead on anything concerning a Cuban paratrooper with a birthmark on his face. That's about all I know..."

"You said the Yucatán," Encizo reminded him. "How'd you know that? Was it labeled in the guy's scrapbook or something?"

"He used to be with Montoya," Alverez explained. "Francisco Montoya, the bandit leader. Montoya's gang spends most of their time hiding in the Yucatán. Besides, I remember this fellow mentioned when they saw these soldiers armed with Communist weapons. He said a couple of his bandit buddies got killed. Said he had a picture of some of the gunmen. He thought they might be terrorists or even Sandinistas. When I saw the birthmark on the soldier in the photo, I thought he might be the man you've been looking for."

"How do I find Montoya?" Encizo demanded.

"I don't know," Alverez answered. "I never dealt with him. *Loco hombre.* Something left over from Pancho Villa's day. I don't do business with crazy people. That's the truth. I swear on my mother's grave."

"How'd you like to meet up with your mom again?" Encizo asked, moving the knife toward Alverez's face. "I ought to do the world a favor and kill you right now."

He wiped the blade of his dagger on Alverez's polo shirt, streaking the white fabric with the henchman's blood. Alverez trembled, but Encizo moved the knife away from the gangster.

"You're lucky I've got an aversion to murder," Encizo stated. "But if you've lied to me, I'll find you, Alverez. Sooner or later I'll catch up with you. I'll find whatever rock you're under at the time and kill you. That's a promise, little thief. Your life is worth too little for me to spare it twice."

"Everything I told you was the truth," Alverez insisted, his head bobbing up and down. "I swear."

"Yeah, sure," Encizo muttered as he used the knife to cut the telephone cord. "We're leaving now. Don't give us any reason to come back."

Encizo and Cassias walked from the warehouse and climbed into the sedan. Cassias started the engine while Encizo opened the briefcase to examine the pictures once more.

"You did good work," Encizo commented. "I didn't know if you were out there or not."

"It was easy," Cassias replied. "No guards outside. I could have come through the front gate instead of cutting through the wire at the north end of the fence. You sure the man in the picture is the one you're been looking for?"

"I'm positive," the Cuban said solemnly. "It's a picture of Captain Raul Encizo. My younger brother."

3

"Okay, fellas," Hal Brognola muttered, the stump of his cigar bobbing in his mouth. He glanced at his wristwatch as he spoke. "May as well take a seat and we'll get started."

"I think we ought to wait a few more minutes for Rafael to arrive," Gary Manning suggested. The big Canadian rolled his shoulders in a massive shrug. "Is it going to hurt if we wait for him before we start?"

"I don't think he's gonna be here today," Brognola answered with a sigh.

"Has something happened to Encizo?" Yakov Katzenelenbogen asked, concern in his voice.

"As far as I know he's okay," the cigar-chewing Fed replied, "but I don't figure he'll show up. That's part of what I gotta talk to you guys about."

Katzenelenbogen nodded and took a seat at the conference table in the Stony Man War Room. He knew Brognola would explain everything during the course of the briefing. The Fed was the chief of operations for Stony Man and the liaison officer for the White House. Brognola not only had to assign duties to the enforcement arms of Stony Man, but he also had to evaluate the tons of intelligence information pouring into the organization from a thousand different sources. Aaron Kurtzman—known as the "Bear"—was the computer wizard who supervised the actual intel gathering, but the real job of the evaluation fell to Brognola, who also assigned Kurtzman most of his priorities.

Brognola did not have an easy job. He had to coordinate virtually every phase of each operation. He had to put together missions and supply the men with equipment. The men of Phoenix Force chose their own weapons and gear, but Brognola had to make certain everything was in stock. He also had to arrange for identification papers, passports, sometimes firearm permits and other items. The Fed generally arranged transportation, frequently on military flights, and connections with other clandestine or security organizations. These included outfits in foreign countries since the majority of Phoenix Force's assignments were outside the United States.

Hal Brognola carried the weight of a world on his shoulders, a world that few people even knew existed. The pressures of his station were enormous, yet he seemed to handle it with gruff ease. The Fed was always there for his men in the field. Phoenix Force could always count on him to be on hand at the headquarters if they needed him during an assignment.

Yakov Katzenelenbogen appreciated the Fed's situation. Katz had been involved with espionage, guerrilla combat and antiterrorism since he was a boy in Europe. His family, Jews of Russian descent, had been wiped out by the Nazis. Young Yakov joined the resistance and fought the Nazis with commandos of the French underground and later the American OSS.

After the war Katz moved to Palestine and joined Israel's war for independence. This led to involvement in subsequent wars, including the Six Day War, where an explosion claimed his right arm and the life of his only son. A master linguist, brilliant strategist and a highly skilled combat veteran, Katz became a colonel in the Israeli Mossad intelligence network. He had also worked with most of the major espionage networks of the free world—American CIA, British SIS, French Sûreté and the West German BND.

Yet Yakov Katzenelenbogen looked more like a college professor than a superspy or a veteran commando. Middle-aged and a bit paunchy at the waist, Katz favored tweed suits and either turtlenecks or pale blue shirts with houndstooth check ties. He made no attempt to conceal his age, and on this occasion had not bothered to fix a prosthetic device to the stump of his right limb. The empty sleeve was pinned back to his right shoulder. The arm had been amputated at the elbow. He had brought along his two favorite prosthetic devices in a case that he placed beside his chair.

"What in bleedin' hell is going on here, Hal?" David McCarter demanded, sticking a Player's cigarette into his mouth. "You know where Rafael is? How about telling the rest of us?"

"I'm sure Hal intends to tell us, David," Katz said in his gentle, reasonable voice. "Give the man a chance."

McCarter shrugged and seemed to crease even more wrinkles into his sport jacket with the gesture. The tall, fox-faced Briton always looked as if he had slept in his clothes and probably tossed and turned all night, as well. McCarter wouldn't win any fashion awards and his sharp tongue and short temper often left a negative impression with people who first met him, but McCarter was a top-notch professional in the field.

A product of the tough East End of London, McCarter was a veteran of the elite British SAS. He had seen action in Northern Ireland, Oman and even in Hong Kong during a special covert "police action." He had also been a "special observer" in Vietnam and participated in Operation Nimrod, the spectacular SAS raid on the Iranian embassy in London in 1980. He thrived on action and seemed most at home on a battlefield. McCarter had been on a lot of battlefields since he joined Phoenix Force and he loved it.

"Okay," Brognola began, striking a wood match to light the end of his cigar. "You guys are aware that Rafael has a brother who's a paratrooper in the Cuban army?"

"Hell, yes," Calvin James declared. "The dude damn near killed Rafael during that mission we had in Colombia about a year and a half ago. I would have shot the guy if Rafael hadn't stopped me."

James was the only native-born American among the men of Phoenix Force. The lanky black warrior had grown up in a ghetto section of the south side of Chicago. His first lessons in survival had been on the streets of his hometown. James was seventeen when he enlisted into the navy and became a hospital corpsman for the elite Seals.

He served in Vietnam and was highly decorated for valor. James had planned to make a career in medicine and chemistry, but his goals changed after the violent death of his mother and the equally tragic death of his younger sister. James joined the San Francisco Police Department and became a member of the SWAT team. He was still a policeman when Phoenix Force drafted him for a mission. James had been with them ever since.

"Yeah," Gary Manning added. "That was when we came up against El Tiburón the cocaine czar and his Cuban allies. Rafael's brother Raul apparently escaped in a helicopter along with the commander of the Cuban forces at El Tiburón's jungle estate."

"Well, Captain Raul Encizo may have surfaced again," Brognola explained. "In Colombia, Raul was part of a training operation, right?"

"Sort of hard to put together all the details about El Tiburón's operation after we blew the hell out of it," Manning said with a shrug.

"You're the expert at blowing the hell out of things, mate," McCarter commented. "You ought to know."

Manning grunted. The muscular Canadian was the team demolitions expert. In fact, Manning was one of the best plastic explosives technicians in the world. It was a skill he had mastered even before he served as a "special observer" with the 5th Special Forces in Nam. He had also been a member of an antiterrorist unit connected with the Royal Canadian Mounted Police.

He had on-the-job training in this field when he was attached to the West German GSG-9, one of the best trained and most professional antiterrorist units in the world. The experience allowed Manning to develop his skills and increase his knowledge. However the RCMP was put out of the covert operations business, and Manning had little opportunity to use his hard-earned abilities. That changed dramatically after he joined Phoenix Force.

"As far as we could put the pieces together after the Colombian mission," Katz began, "Raul Encizo was instructing troops and El Tiburón's hired thugs in hand-to-hand combat and probably small arms and fundamental combat tactics.''

''Well, there's a good chance he's training left-wing terrorists in Mexico,'' Brognola stated. ''Recent intelligence sources suggest there's a big training operation going on in the Yucatán peninsula, which involves at least fifty 23rd September Communist League terrorists. Fanatic pro-Castro types.''

''Cuban paratroopers are training these dudes?'' Calvin James inquired. ''Is that based on conclusive evidence?''

''It's a little shaky,'' the Fed answered. ''One of the sources came from police informers in Mexico City, who supposedly got the story from some bandits or dope smugglers or something like that. According to the story, the terrorists and the Cubans opened fire on the crooks when they ran across each other's operations in the Yucatán. The story probably would have been dismissed entirely if some fisherman along the gulf hadn't found a man's body washed up on the shore. He was identified as a schoolteacher from Minnesota who was in Mexico on vacation. Hold on a second....''

Brognola gathered up a folder and opened it to check the information of the reports from Mexico.

''Here it is,'' he announced. ''The man's name was Robert Newton. He went into the Yucatán with an archaeologist named Gerald Harrimon. I guess they were looking for Aztec treasure or something like that. Anyway, neither man had been heard of after they went off into the jungle. Harrimon's family contacted the embassy in Mexico City to try to locate him. There is still nothing definite on Harrimon, but they did find the body of an old guy the two Americans had hired as a guide. Divers found his corpse in the gulf. It had been weighted down with rocks. Apparently the same procedure had been followed in Newton's case, but his body still floated up and drifted to shore."

"I take it they didn't drown," Katz remarked, taking out a pack of Camels.

"Newton had been beaten to death," the Fed explained. "Pretty vicious beating, according to the autopsy. The M.E. in Mexico City wrote a comment—which fortunately has been translated into English—about what he thinks might be the cause of death. He says Newton's body resembled corpses he'd seen before: victims of gang violence who had been stomped to death. He figures somebody literally kicked Newton's head in."

"Nasty," Manning agreed, "but it doesn't prove that Cubans or terrorists were involved."

"No," Brognola replied. "But the old man, known only by the name Ramon, was a harmless derelict type who worked just to get enough money so he could stay drunk for a few days. He had been shot with an automatic rifle. Good marksmanship. Got him right in the heart with three rounds. One bullet was still in the body. It was a 7.62 mm slug. Ballistics confirm it was fired by a Kalashnikov rifle.''

"And the AK-47 is standard issue for the Cuban military,'' Manning said with a nod. "Still, that doesn't mean Raul Encizo is among the Cubans involved in the incident.''

"Let me finish,'' Brognola insisted. "The stoolie who told the *federales* about the Cuban soldiers with the terrorists claimed that a bandit witness described one of the Cuban officers as a muscle-bound guy with a 'red blot' on his face. Rafael recognized his brother in Colombia because of a birthmark on his face. Heart-shaped and strawberry-colored, right? I'd say it sounds like Raul.''

"How the hell did Rafael find out this stuff?'' Calvin James inquired. "If he's headed down to Mexico already, he must have found out around the same time the information reached Kurtzman's computers.''

"We all had a life before Phoenix Force,'' Katz stated. "Rafael doesn't talk much about the past, but we know he used to help federal agents with drug dealers and other criminals from south of the border. He probably established contacts with individuals involved in the Mexican underworld. Just the way you knew informers among the criminal element when you were a policeman in San Francisco and I knew double agents who sold information to either side when I was with Mossad. Rafael has probably been in touch with some of his old sources ever since we returned from Colombia.''

"Ever since he knew his brother was alive and a member of Castro's army,'' Manning added grimly.

"Damn it to hell,'' McCarter muttered as he started to pace the floor by the table. "He should have told us about this. We're partners, damn it.''

"He didn't tell us because if he did we would have either tried to stop him or gone to Mexico with him,'' Katz explained. "Rafael sees this as a personal problem. It concerns himself and his brother. I'm sure he doesn't want to get Phoenix Force involved in a family matter.''

"Family matter?'' James scoffed. "Maybe Rafael figures blood is thicker than water, but I wouldn't count on Raul sharing that notion. Raul has been taken to education centers to be brainwashed by the Communists since he was five years old. They've had about twenty-eight years to work on his head. Raul's a blasted killing machine. I saw him in action. If Rafael gets careless because of sentiment, that dude will wipe him out.''

"Rafael can take care of himself pretty well, too,'' McCarter declared, more to reassure himself than to convince the others.

"He's not going to kill his own brother,'' Gary Manning stated. "You know that as well as I do.

Even in self-defense he wouldn't do it. He'd rather let his brother kill him than the other way around."

"Gary's right," Katz agreed. "You called us in here to tell us about this, Hal. What do you want us to do?"

"Hell," Brognola snorted, as he shoved the cigar into the corner of his mouth. "I know you guys. We've been working together for a few years now, and I got some idea how you hotshots operate. If I hadn't told you about this, you would have found out through your own clever little sources anyway. Then you four would be on your way to Mexico on another unauthorized mission. You've done it before, so don't bullshit me that you wouldn't do it this time."

"You could have sent us on a mission on the other side of the world instead of telling us about Rafael," Manning remarked with a thin smile.

"I don't have anything for you on the other side of the world right now," the Fed replied with mock gruffness. "Look, the President hasn't sanctioned a mission into Mexico, but I can cover that. After all, at least one, probably two U.S. citizens have been murdered by Cuban-connected leftist terrorists. Obviously the 23rd SCL is involved in a plan to try to take over Mexico. I doubt if they're really any closer to succeeding than they have been in the past, but there's no need to tell the President that. The possi-

bility of a Communist takeover in Mexico is reason
enough for us to be concerned."

"So you're officially sending us on a mission to
Mexico?" McCarter asked eagerly.

"Yeah," Brognola answered with a sigh. "I figure it's better to do it this way. At least you guys will
stay in touch so I have some idea what's going on.
Officially, your mission is to find the terrorist operation and put it out of business, but go right ahead
and concentrate on finding Encizo. When you catch
up with him, decide what to do—take out the terrorists, help him contact his brother or just bring him
back here. If you can do all three that would be
great."

"We'll do our best," Katz assured him with a
smile. "Without White House sanction we can't
expect any help from the Mexican authorities, can
we?"

"Afraid not," Brognola replied. "In fact, if they
catch you running around with guns or explosives the
federales will probably throw your butts in prison. If
that happens, we can probably get you out by working through the embassy, but it would sure cause a lot
of problems for Stony Man. The President might
even order that Phoenix Force be dismantled if that
happens. So try not to get caught."

"Will we be entirely on our own?" James asked.

"Pretty close, but not quite," the Fed answered,
once again checking his notes. "The Bear came up

with the name of a cutout operative in Mexico City. A fellow named Ricardo Vasquez. He's worked for the CIA several times in the past. Private espionage free-lancer, but always works for American and pro-Democracy interests. Vasquez is reliable, and he has lots of information sources, including where you guys can get weapons and explosives. Better if you get those items after you arrive in Mexico and buy the stuff through Vasquez. You're not going to be able to smuggle much weaponry or ammo on a commercial flight to Mexico."

"We understand," Katz said with a nod. "And thanks, Hal."

"Yeah," Brognola said with an almost embarrassed shrug. "Just remember that this mission is for real, with just as much risk as any other. In some ways there are even more than usual. Oh, one more thing before you leave. If you go down there and Encizo has been swallowed up and vanished from the face of the earth, bear in mind I'd rather the rest of you guys came back in one piece than get yourselves blown away trying to find out what happened. If it comes to that, I'd rather lose one member of Phoenix Force than all five."

4

Major Julio Pescador could have stood being happier. He had hoped he had seen the last of jungles and guerrilla combat missions after he returned to Cuba following a less than satisfactory operation in Colombia. Havana was angry and disappointed by the failure, but Pescador had managed to convince his superiors that El Tiburón's carelessness had ruined the mission.

Pescador's hope of a promotion to colonel had been smashed by the disaster in Colombia, yet things could have gone far worse. He was not court-martialed or even reprimanded, although every man under his command, except Captain Encizo, had been killed during a battle at El Tiburón's headquarters. That mission had been a high-risk proposition from the start. Working with a cocaine syndicate had brought an undisciplined, greedy lot into the operation. It should not have surprised anyone that it had failed when the Cuban soldiers had to work with unprincipled gangsters interested only in profit.

Pescador was a dutiful parrot of Castro's Leninist-Marxist version of communism. He quoted all the current party slogans and supported the international workers' revolution against the capitalist oppressors. The major did not necessarily believe all the rhetoric, but he learned it was best to give lip service to the doctrines of Havana. Basically, Pescador believed most of the tenets of the *Communist Manifesto*, yet he was forty-one years old and past the age of fiery youthful enthusiasm. Pescador was less interested in the success of the revolution than simply living out the rest of his life without running afoul of the government and winding up in prison or in front of a firing squad. He had a family in Santa Clara: a wife, two sons and a daughter.

His eldest son and daughter were married and had children of their own. Pescador had yet to see his grandchildren, and now Havana had sent him to Mexico to yet another tropical jungle. They said he had experience in such missions and, if the Colombian assignment had truly failed because of El Tiburón, he ought to be able to handle the mission in Mexico.

Havana had even teamed Pescador with Captain Raul Encizo again. The major was not thrilled about the arrangement, either, although Raul Encizo was an impressive commando. The captain certainly had courage and a variety of skills to go with it. He was intelligent, dedicated, an expert in small arms, survival techniques and guerrilla warfare. The junior officer was in superb physical condition and had a 2nd dan black belt in karate.

But Raul Encizo was also a fanatic. Pescador knew a bit about the man's background. The Party had taken him to a special education unit and drummed propaganda and Marxist philosophy into him until the messages were coming out his ears. The state then had decided that a bright, physically strong youth could best serve the Republic of Cuba in the military. Actually he had been trained since childhood for that purpose. However, the state had been so pleased with the results that it had failed to realize when the training had gone too far.

The captain had been overconditioned, like a guard dog that was too eager to attack. He didn't care about anything except killing enemies of the state and instructing others how to accomplish that goal. He wanted to die for the glory of the Communist revolution, and he expected everyone under his command to share his dedication. He was fearless in the face of danger. No rational man is without fear.

Pescador watched a typical example of that extremist behavior as he stared out the window of the crudely built headquarters building at their base in the Yucatán. Captain Encizo was teaching a crash course in unarmed combat to a group of 23rd SCL recruits.

"Un hombre tan estúpido," Pescador muttered, shaking his head.

The major considered the notion of teaching those recruits jujitsu and karate to be a waste of time. Mastery of the martial arts required time and discipline. There was little enough time for training the terrorists in the use of firearms, explosives, escape and evasion techniques, camouflage and communications and other skills. Hand-to-hand combat training was a waste of that precious time in Pescador's opinion.

Of course, Major Pescador knew that Captain Encizo viewed things differently. Martial arts training had helped provide the discipline that was the backbone of his life, so he assumed it would help the terrorists become better fighting men, more controlled and confident on the battlefield. He did not understand the purpose of supporting the terrorists. Havana had not sent them to Mexico to turn the 23rd SCL into an efficient fighting unit. They were terrorists, not soldiers.

The terrorists were young zealots, violent idealists who were dedicated to tearing down the present government of Mexico, but they did not really know what would replace it after it was torn down. That did not matter. Their politics gave them justification to commit acts of violence. They claimed the destruction they created was for the sake of a noble revolution, to liberate the masses and bring equality to all people, yet it was the destruction itself that they thrived on. As for liberating the masses, Pescador thought with contempt, the majority of their victims would be unarmed civilians. They murdered their own people and then boasted of how they intended to save them from the oppressive government they planned to overthrow.

Havana did not really want them to succeed in their ultimate goal. What would Cuba have to gain by allowing a pack of mad dogs to take control of Mexico? The Soviets probably wouldn't want that, either, and given their influence with Fidel Castro, their desires carried a lot of weight.

The 23rd SCL was getting support from Havana because the terrorists would help set the stage for the real revolution in the future. The theories behind the strategy were explained in Carlos Marighella's *The Terrorist Classic: Manual of the Urban Guerrilla*. Havana thought so much of the book that thousands of copies had been printed and distributed to terrorist cell leaders throughout Central and South America. The manual had been translated into French, Italian, Turkish and English. Havana shipped them out to pro-Marxist extremist groups in other countries to assist in the "revolution" throughout the world.

Major Pescador wiped his moon-shaped face with a damp cloth as he watched Captain Encizo demonstrate how to apply a simple wristlock by twisting the opponent's hand and forearm in different directions. Pescador was miserable in the heat and humidity of the jungle. Even with an electric fan pointed at his face and a cold bottle of beer from an ice chest in his office, the weather was difficult to tolerate. Yet there was the captain, tirelessly instructing his pupils in self-defense in a sawdust-covered clearing beneath the hot afternoon sun.

"I'd like you to teach me that trick, *Capitán*," Jesus Morales requested with a broad grin on his lean bearded face.

"If you please," Captain Encizo replied, gesturing for Jesus to step forward.

José Morales, Jesus's brother, giggled as his sibling approached Raul Encizo. The Morales brothers had been born and raised in a tough slum environment in Tijuana. They had worked together in street crime since they were teenagers. The brothers had bashed a lot of heads, kicked in countless ribs and cut a few throats during their youthful careers.

They had joined the 23rd SCL because they figured the terrorist outfit was some sort of scam. The SCL occasionally financed its operations by robbing banks and knocking over armored cars. It seemed a profitable venture to the Morales brothers, but so far they had been disappointed. Lectures on politics, military drills and lessons in improvised sanitation techniques in the field bored them to tears. They had not enlisted to listen to officers, whom they

considered snot-nosed college boys, rant about the
evils of capitalism or learn how to march like a toy
soldier or dig latrines like *peónes*. They wanted to
know when the hell they would stop playing games
and decide to rob a bank.

Jose watched with narrow-eyed interest, knowing
something amusing was bound to happen. The *cubano* turd thought he was going to teach them how
to fight? Maybe he could show them how to use automatic rifles and grenades, but instruct them in this
Oriental bullshit? *¡Estúpido!* The Morales brothers
had been in enough street fights to know how to take
care of themselves.

Jesus Morales stepped toward Captain Encizo and
raised his right fist. The Cuban officer stood with his
feet balanced and hands poised as if imitating the
stance of a cat waiting to strike. Jesus almost laughed
in his face. He would show the *cubano* a lesson he
learned on the streets of TJ when he was a kid. Jesus started to throw a right cross in slow motion, fist
inching toward Encizo's face at a pace suited for
demonstration rather than actual combat. The captain started to raise his arms.

Suddenly Jesus lashed out a boot at the Cuban's
groin. He would have been gratified to feel his foot
connect with his target and see the captain rolling
around on the ground holding his *cojones* while the
others laughed at his plight and cheered Jesus for his
boldness and cleverness.

But his boot missed the target.

Captain Encizo had seen the shift of Jesus's shoulders and realized the Mexican punk was about to throw a kick. He moved out of the path of the attack and Jesus's foot whirled through the air. Morales nearly lost his balance, then flapped with his arms like a clumsy bird as he tried to keep his footing.

With his right leg Raul Encizo hooked a hard kick to Jesus's left kidney. The Mexican groaned and fell to the sawdust-covered ground. The onlookers laughed, just as he had fantasized, but they were laughing at his humiliation at the hands of the Cuban.

Boiling with rage, Jesus grabbed a fistful of sawdust and scrambled to his feet. Captain Encizo calmly waited for him to rise, arms folded on his chest. Instead of mocking or threatening him, the Cuban simply appeared bored by the confrontation.

"¡Cabrón!" Jesus Morales snarled as he threw the sawdust at Encizo's face and swung a right cross with all his force behind it.

Captain Encizo ducked, and the sawdust missed his face to land harmlessly in his hair. Morales had expected the sawdust to fly into Raul's eyes and mouth. His opponent was supposed to be half-blind and gagging before his fist streaked out at the Cuban's head. Things just were not going as Jesus had planned.

Dodging the oncoming blow, the captain grabbed the punk's wrist. He yanked Jesus forward and whipped a knee into his abdomen. Morales doubled up with a moaning gasp and Raul chopped the side of his hand across the base of his skull. The Mexican fell to his knees, stunned by the blow. Moving behind him, Raul slammed a heel-kick between Jesus's shoulder blades. The kick knocked the Mexican street kid facedown into the sawdust.

"When you get an opponent down," Encizo told his students in a calm voice, "you make certain he stays down."

The captain suddenly bent his knees and landed on Jesus. One of his knees was shoved into the nape of Jesus's neck, pushing his face deeper in the sawdust while the other was planted under his shoulder blades. Smothering in the sawdust, Jesus struggled to free himself but the officer easily kept him pinned and simply pushed down on the fallen man's triceps to prevent him from getting any leverage with his arms. The Mexican punk's legs thrashed uselessly and kicked the ground in desperation.

"Jesus!" José Morales cried as he watched his brother helplessly struggle for his life. "You're killing him!"

"Si," Captain Encizo confirmed. "That's how you deal with an enemy. You kill him."

"Right!" José exclaimed as he took the knife from his pocket. He pressed the button on his switchblade and four inches of sharp steel snapped into place. José charged for Encizo, determined to kill the man who threatened to smother his brother to death. Captain Encizo clenched his fist and smashed a *seiken* karate punch to the base of Jesus's skull before he jumped to his feet to deal with the other attacker.

"*¡Alto!*" Major Pescador cried as he raced from the headquarters to the training area. "Stop! This has gone far enough!"

But the situation had already gone too far to be stopped by words. José attacked Captain Encizo with a slash that revealed more desperation and anger than skill. Raul Encizo dodged the wild swipe and delivered a foot-sword kick to his opponent's wrist. The knife flew from numb fingers. The terrible pain in José's wrist told him the bone had been broken.

Captain Encizo swung a fast roundhouse kick. His boot crashed into the side of José's head. Morales staggered and started to fall, but Encizo grabbed his opponent with one hand and pumped a karate punch to José's solar plexus. The Mexican's body jerked from the force of the blow, which also made him wheeze like a sick horse. José's knees buckled, and he began to sag to the ground. Pescador shouted for Encizo to stop, but the captain ignored him.

Raul Encizo seized his opponent by the shirt and slashed a karate chop to his collarbone. The Mexican hood doubled over from the blow, and Encizo drove a powerful knee kick under the stunned man's sternum. José Morales trembled violently and dropped to the ground. His twitching body thrashed about in the sawdust and then lay still.

"Damn it, Captain," Pescador complained, "I told you to stop."

"I had to finish him, Comrade Major," Encizo replied without apology. "It was necessary not only to ensure my own life, but as a lesson to the men."

The cheering and laughter of the students had ceased. Neither of the Morales brothers stirred. Two of the terrorist students ventured forward and checked them for signs of life. They found none.

"You killed them, *Capitán*," one of the men announced in a stunned voice. "You killed them both."

"Of course," Encizo answered. "I hope you all paid attention and learned from it. If a man attacks you in earnest, you destroy him. Both of these men would still be alive if they had regarded this as a training session. Instead of taking advantage of the opportunity to learn, the first man turned the lesson into a duel. He lost."

"I don't think Jesus intended to kill you," a terrorist named Lamelas stated, shaking his head sadly. "The Morales brothers were hot-blooded young men. They were a bit foolish, but..."

"Never assume that a man who attacks you does not intend to take your life," Captain Encizo insisted. "The first man came at me twice. I would have spared him if he had learned his lesson and hadn't resumed the attack. The second man had a weapon. He clearly intended to cause serious injury or kill me. True, his attack was clumsy. Emotion got the better of him and he wielded the knife like a fool."

"José was trying to save his brother," Lamelas insisted. "Of course he was emotional after he saw what you'd done to his brother...."

"His emotion did not save his brother, it only cost him his own life, as well," Captain Encizo declared with a shrug. "He was an idiot to risk his life for his brother's sake. There is no family except the family of the brotherhood of our revolution. Any other loyalty is treason."

The majority of the men standing around were disturbed by Captain Encizo's callous attitude, but Pedro Garcia was simply amused. He remembered the captain's disapproval of Garcia's and his comrades' method of dealing with the two Americans and their guide, yet the man thought nothing of killing two of their own and justifying it by claiming it was for the edification of the new recruits. Raul Encizo was an interesting paradox, Garcia thought. More machine than man. A machine that killed without hesitation and found methods more objectionable than reasons.

"I think this training period is over, Captain," Major Pescador said grimly. "Unless you feel like killing someone else."

"Not at the moment, Comrade Major," Encizo replied in a perfectly serious voice. He was not being sarcastic.

5

Tijuana is one of the best known cities in all of Mexico. It is probably the most frequently visited by citizens of the United States because of its location right across the border from California. "TJ" is a popular city for a number of reasons, among them the fact that thousands of items of merchandise can be purchased in Tijuana for much less than in the U.S.

Some people travel to TJ in search of certain types of "merchandise" they have difficulty finding in the States. Tijuana had long ago established its reputation as an "open city," where drugs were readily available. For many years it was the unofficial "capital of marijuana dealers" and a major center for heroin traffic into the United States. Though a lot of drug deals are still made in Tijuana, TJ couldn't keep pace with times. The dope scene had changed over the years. Most marijuana in the U.S. was now homegrown, and cocaine had taken over as the most popular drug for those individuals bent on wrecking their lives. The South American syndicates ran the "coke" action now, favoring Miami to the California border for the port of U.S. entry.

But Tijuana is still popular for another type of drug trade—narcotics. Many types of "prescription" medication—barbiturates, stimulants and codeine products—are sold over the counter in Mexican pharmacies. While the majority of American customers purchasing these items don't intend to abuse the drugs—some are cancer victims looking for accessible, affordable relief from the pain—many others simply take advantage of the casual pharmaceutical policies and low prices to stock up on medication.

Although the fabled "donkey shows" are no longer practiced in TJ—at least not as prominently as in the past, although according to rumors such curious performances can still be witnessed if advance arrangements are made—there are still plenty of legal strip shows, topless bars and brothels. Though technically illegal, the whorehouses are generally ignored by the *federales*. Enterprising cabdrivers look for *yanquis* among the passersby on the streets and ask if they would like to see a "private show."

Tijuana has been called a "dirty little city," a bottom-of-the-barrel version of Las Vegas. To whatever degree that may be true, the blame for TJ's sleazy taint lies with the *norteamericanos* more than the *mexicanos* who live there. The nastier busi-

nesses—legal, illegal and somewhere in between—
thrive because of the large number of American
tourists coming to the city in search of such things.

Rafael Encizo had been to Tijuana on previous
occasions, but his last visit had been years before.
This time he was accompanied by Manual Cassias,
who drove the old Ford sedan through the crowded
cobblestone streets. The traffic was always heavy in
TJ. It was rather similar to the traffic typical of New
York City. Cars bullied each other for space on
streets designed for the calmer and less congested
days of the 1940s. The vehicles ended up bumper-to-
bumper, but occasionally managed a frenzied bolt
through yellow lights or from one lane to another.
Remarkably the number of accidents were compar-
atively few.

Tijuana did not look quite the way Encizo remembered it. The U.S. influence had changed the
appearance of the city. It seemed less Spanish. Two
familiar golden arches loomed above the rooftop of
a fast-food restaurant. Most of the buildings had a
generic modern appearance that revealed little of the
Spanish heritage except for the advertisements plastered across walls and mounted on billboards. Some
traditional adobe structures remained, and a few
cantinas retained a Spanish flavor instead of adopt-
ing the beer-joint, hangout style typical of taverns in
the U.S.

Merchants with blankets, pottery and other items carried their commodities in their arms and accosted passing vehicles to try to make a quick sale. Pawnshop owners stood in front of their establishments ready to spew tales of the wondrous bargains to be had right then and there. Beggars in tatters and wearing Indian blankets wandered the streets with hands outstretched, their faces gaunt, eyes looking empty and hopeless.

The *federales* also patrolled the streets. Mexican police had a reputation for being tough, sometimes corrupt and occasionally trigger-happy. Encizo knew that there was a certain amount of truth to those claims. Many *federales* supplemented their incomes by taking bribes. Some also had a scam using real or trumped-up charges to shake the *touristes* down for whatever might be on them and perhaps confiscating valuable personal property, as well. Even high-ranking officers had been known to indulge in such uniformed piracy.

Encizo realized that the claims of widespread police corruption in Mexico were somewhat exaggerated, but such things happened often enough to be taken seriously, especially in Tijuana. They would have to avoid the *federales*. Encizo was going to break enough laws to spend the rest of his life in a Mexican prison if the police found out what he was up to.

"You've never met Benito, have you?" Cassias inquired as he steered the car off the main street and headed toward the Tijuana bullring.

"No," Encizo replied, a bit wearily because he had already answered the question twice before. "But you told me about him."

"Oh, yeah," Cassias sighed. "I remember now. Sorry. We'll be there soon. Benito used to be a matador and he likes to operate near the bullring. You an aficionado of the sport?"

"Not really," Encizo confessed. "I'll admit it takes a lot of courage to be a bullfighter, but I can't help feeling sorry for the bull. It wasn't the animal's idea to get into the fight business. Maybe I just see too much bloodshed in my line of work to want to see more of it for entertainment."

"Well, don't criticize bullfighting in front of Benito," Cassias urged, watching the road with one eye as he tried to scan the surrounding buildings with the other. "He's pretty sensitive about the subject."

"I didn't come here to talk about bullfighting with Benito Tillo," Encizo assured him. "I'm only interested in his current profession."

"Just bear it in mind when you meet him," Cassias stated, turning the steering wheel to swing into the narrow parking space before a row of small buildings. "We have arrived, Rafael."

Cassias parked the sedan by a leather-goods shop that was flanked by an auto-parts store and a cantina. The leather-goods shop was the smallest establishment of the lot, but it was also the most important because it was Benito Tillo's base. The other buildings were actually owned by Tillo and the businesses they housed were operated by family members and friends.

Encizo and Cassias entered the leather shop. It did not look like much. Belts, purses, wallets, jackets, shoes and bullwhips were displayed on shelves and hung from wall pegs. Several old posters announced bullfights featuring the matador Benito Tillo.

"Buenos días," the man behind the counter greeted them with a grin. "I've been expecting you, Manuel. This must be your mysterious friend. Sanchez, right?"

"Or Rafael," Encizo said with a shrug. "Either will do, depending on how you prefer to do business."

"A pleasure to meet you, Rafael," Tillo said with a nod. "Manuel could not tell me much on the telephone, but I understand this is something special. Let me close the shop to be sure we can discuss business in private."

Tillo stepped from behind the counter and limped slightly as he crossed the room to the door. He had been badly gored on several occasions during his career as a bullfighter, and he had a steel pin in his left hip. Tillo was a tall, thin man who appeared to be in fairly good physical condition despite his past injuries.

He locked the door and pulled down the blinds on the windows. He switched on a burglar-alarm system wired to the door and windows before he led the two visitors into the back room of his shop.

Yanking back a curtain, Tillo revealed a steel vault with a combination lock. He jealously guarded the numbers and sequence to the combination and shielded the view from Cassias and Encizo as he worked the dial. Tillo opened the vault. It contained a variety of handguns, revolvers and semiautomatic pistols. Some were Mexican-manufactured weapons, others originated from South or Central America. Most had been imported from the United States. The guns were clean, freshly oiled and many appeared to be new. Encizo noticed there were no boxes of ammunition stored in the vault. Tillo clearly did not intend to set up a potential attempt for somebody to rob him with one of his own weapons.

The former matador was a gunrunner. He generally sold guns to markets outside Mexico, but he also did business with a few smugglers like Cassias, whom he regarded as businessmen like himself, operating just outside the law to pursue an individualistic version of free enterprise.

Tillo considered himself to be a patriot, and he was strongly opposed to communism. He sold a lot of arms to Contra outfits in Central America. Cassias had assured Encizo that Tillo could be trusted to sell weapons at a reasonable price and not betray them to either the authorities or any leftist group that might contact and alert the Cuban and 23rd SCL terrorists in the Yucatán.

"I don't see any Heckler & Koch pistols," Encizo said with a frown. "No Smith & Wesson M-59 auto-loaders, either."

"I thought you were in love with the Walther PPK," Cassias remarked.

"I switched to 9 mm pistols some time ago," the Cuban answered. "I still carry a PPK .380 for backup, but I've generally used an H&K for my regular sidearm. For a while I used an M-59, but Heckler & Koch weapons are my favorite. You wouldn't have have any MP-5s in stock, would you?"

"Machine guns?" Tillo raised his thick eyebrows. "Manuel told me you would be a serious customer."

"You have submachine guns?" Encizo asked.

"Of course," Tillo confirmed. "Mostly Mendoza submachine guns and a few M-3s made in the United States."

"The old .45-caliber grease gun?" The Cuban made a face. "No thanks. What caliber are the Mendoza subguns?"

"I have some in .45 and the others are 9 mm parabellums," the gunrunner declared. "Now, if you want 9 mm pistols, I suggest you get the submachine guns in the same caliber. Have you ever fired a Mendoza?''

"It's similar to the old Thompson submachine gun," Encizo answered, examining the handgun selection more carefully. "The Mendoza is a fine weapon."

He removed a compact matte-black pistol with polymer plastic grips and a bobbed hammer. Encizo nodded with self-congratulation when he confirmed that the pistol was a Ruger P-85. The Cuban had fired such pistols at the Stony Man shooting range. The P-85 was a fairly recent development by Storm, Ruger & Company. It was a well-made, sturdy and dependable weapon. A double-action autoloader with a 15-round capacity, the P-85 handled quite well at the range. Encizo's only complaint about the Ruger was that the pistol was not accurate beyond 25 yards. However, since most handgun battles were fought within five to twenty feet, it wasn't a serious argument against the Ruger.

"You've selected the P-85," Tillo noticed. "Good choice. I just got some of those pistols last week. Not many of them on the black market, you know, but I have resourceful friends in the United States."

"I'm sticking with my old standby," Cassias announced, taking a .357 S&W revolver from the rack. "I don't trust automatics. Too apt to jam, if you ask me."

"Fine," Encizo said with a shrug. "You have any prejudices against submachine guns?"

"I've never fired one, Rafael," Cassias admitted. "Maybe I should stick with something I know how to handle. A lever-action or bolt-action rifle maybe. Or a pump shotgun if you figure that would be better."

"We'll be in a jungle region," Encizo stated. "If we have to fight, it'll probably be fairly close quarters, and odds are you won't get a nice clear target. The wide pattern of buckshot is better for such situations than bolt- or lever-action rifles."

"I have a number of Winchester pump shotguns," Tillo announced. "You intend to participate in some sort of armed assault, Manuel? That is unusual for you. I thought you tried to avoid violence. You've always refused to even smuggle guns across the border for me."

"This is special, Benito," Cassias told him. "I have a personal reason to do this, although the national security and freedom of Mexico are also at stake."

"Is this true?" the gunrunner demanded. "What is this threat? I am a loyal, patriotic Mexican citizen. I think I should know if something threatens my beloved country."

"I'm afraid we can't explain any details," Encizo declared, casting a disapproving glance at Cassias. His friend had already told the gunrunner more than he should have. "This is something of a personal matter."

"A personal matter that concerns the safety of my country?" Tillo frowned. "*My* country, I remind you. Manuel, you are a fine man and I know you love Mexico as the land of your heritage, but you were still born in the United States. Rafael, you speak Spanish fluently and you've even perfected a pretty convincing Mexican accent, but I notice a few words that are not often used by Mexicans and your accent slips a bit. Then it sounds more like the Spanish of the Dominican Republic or perhaps Puerto Rico."

"You have a good ear," Encizo told him. "I'm originally from Cuba, but that was a long time ago."

"You're not a Communist?" Tillo demanded.

"That's why I left Cuba," Encizo said with a sigh. "Look, Benito, all we want are some weapons, ammo and some information about Montoya."

"The *bandido*?" Tillo raised his eyebrows. "Montoya usually operates in the Yucatán area. That must be the jungle you spoke of. . . . Wait! I remember Montoya had some men who claimed they were attacked by mercenaries of some sort in the jungle. In fact, they said some of these men were Cuban soldiers."

"*¡Cristo!*" Cassias cursed. "You are not going to accuse me or Rafael of being Communists? You have known me for many years, Benito. Do you think I would change so much or support Communist invaders from Cuba?''

"Of course not," Tillo assured him. "You are a black marketer and thus a capitalist by anybody's definition. I know you must be going to the Yucatán to fight these Cuban scum. No offense, Rafael."

"None taken," Encizo assured him. "If you'll just cooperate with us, Benito . . ."

"I will do better than that." The gunrunner paused and his chest expanded with pride. "I shall accompany you on this mission."

"We appreciate the offer," the Cuban began, "but I'm afraid that simply isn't possible."

"Why not?" Tillo demanded. "I am not too old. I am probably a few years younger than you, and I have proved my courage in the bullring. Have you ever faced nine hundred kilos of snarling fury? A creature of solid muscle and rage armed with great sharp horns and hoofs? Have you ever stared death in the face with only a cape and a sword?"

"I never had that experience," Encizo admitted, "but I've seen death up close in many other ways. I've seen it in the barrel of a gun and on the blade of a knife. I've seen it in a prison cell and while I was strapped to a chair in a torture chamber. The enemy we're seeking doesn't paw the ground and charge with its head down so one can stab it with a sword and pierce its heart. You have much bravery, my friend. Yet courage is not enough against such opponents."

"I am very good with guns, Rafael," Tillo insisted. "Why do you think I deal in them? Besides, I can get others to help us. I have many friends in this city and beyond. I can also take you to Montoya."

"He has a point, Rafael," Cassias stated with a sigh.

"I want to come," Tillo said, his tone almost pleading. "A man needs challenge to truly feel like a man. I have never truly felt alive since I was forced to retire from the ring. Life is very dull unless one can put it in jeopardy from time to time."

"You don't have to prove your machismo to anyone," Encizo told him. "In fact, if you feel you need some sort of test to prove to yourself that you still have courage, this isn't it. Such an attitude would endanger not only your life but ours, as well. There will be no glory, no cheering crowds, no recognition for one's actions in battle. To be honest, I have a personal reason for being here. The safety of your country is important to me, but that isn't the reason I'm here. I don't even know how great the threat to Mexico might be. My main concern is a family matter."

"I still want to come," Tillo insisted. "I can help. You may, in fact, find your mission into the Yucatán impossible without my help."

"We really could use him, Rafael," Cassias added.

"All right," Encizo agreed reluctantly. He turned to Tillo. "But if you come with us you'll have to follow orders. No independent heroics. You do what you're told and don't give me any crap about it. Anyone you want to recruit, check with us first. I want to know everything there is to know about anybody we take into the jungle. If I veto a choice, that's final. Agreed?"

"Agreed," Tillo said with a nod. He limped to a small refrigerator, opened it and removed three chilled cans of Carta Blanca beer. "Shall we seal our new partnership with a toast?"

"Sure." Encizo managed a smile although he personally considered Carta Blanca to be a bit bland.

"To friendships and victory," Tillo announced, yanking the tab from a beer can.

"And family reunions," Cassias added, placing a hand on Encizo's shoulder. "God willing, we shall find your brother, amigo."

"I just hope we don't get killed in the process," Encizo replied grimly as he lifted his beer can in a toast.

6

Mexico City is the capital of the country. It is also the largest city in Mexico—second largest metropolitan area in the western hemisphere—with a huge, modern international airport to the east. The four Phoenix Force members deplaned at the airport. Ricardo Vasquez met them at Gate 23. He had no trouble recognizing the new arrivals because Katz, Manning, James and McCarter wore identical blue blazers with the initials Y.I. in gold letters on the crests sewn to the breast pockets.

Phoenix Force were traveling as members of the Yardton Institute, a private foundation based in New York City that concentrated on combating illiteracy throughout the world in general, and North and Central America in particular. The organization was regarded by most as well-meaning if largely ineffective. Its membership was comprised of educators, sociologists and assorted humanitarians financed by private funds.

There was nothing suspicious about four Y.I. members flying to Mexico City. The four Phoenix

Force pros had excellent forged identification papers, passports and visas. The Y.I. blazers labeled them as harmless as they passed through customs. Vasquez calmly waited for the four strangers to collect their luggage.

"Welcome to Mexico, gentlemen," he announced with a curt nod. "I hope you had a pleasant flight."

"Very nice, thank you," Yakov Katzenelenbogen assured him, extending his left hand.

Vasquez shook it. He had been told the senior member of the group had an artificial right arm. Katz wore a pair of pearl-gray gloves. Vasquez noticed that the right appeared quite lifelike, but the fingers were rigid and the Israeli kept that arm close to his side to avoid making stiff puppetlike gestures with the prosthesis. Katz was not self-conscious about the synthetic limb, he simply wanted to avoid attracting attention.

"I have a car," Vasquez explained as they moved through the crowded corridors of the airport. "We can talk better when we get there."

"Good idea," Gary Manning agreed, tucking a suitcase under an arm so he could free his hands for carrying a briefcase and another suitcase.

The Canadian was glad Vasquez spoke English. Manning was fluent in French and German, but he only spoke a smattering of Spanish. He noticed Vasquez had mastered English quite well and had even managed to acquire a nondescript Midwest accent, the type favored by network newscasters in America.

It was too early to form a firm opinion of Vasquez. He was young, late twenties or early thirties, but he seemed to be a veteran of covert operations. Vasquez appeared to be an "average man"—medium build, average height and a plain face with bland features. He was neither short nor tall, thin nor fat, handsome nor ugly. This "average" appearance had no doubt helped him in his career as a cutout for the Company. Vasquez was the sort of man who wouldn't stand out in a crowd and anyone trying to describe him would probably use expressions like "average guy" or "he just looked like anybody else." Nature had given Vasquez a form of camouflage for the shadowy profession he had become involved with.

Vasquez led them to his car in the parking lot. It was a Chevy station wagon, big enough for both luggage and passengers. Everything and everyone was loaded into the vehicle before Vasquez spoke again.

"I don't have many details about your mission," he began, starting the engine. "I understand it isn't really connected with regular CIA operations here so I haven't told any of my Company contacts at the U.S. Embassy about this business. You want to keep it that way for now?"

"Absolutely," Katz confirmed. "Do you have a safehouse set up yet?"

"Yes," Vasquez answered. "I also have your weapons and some other gear stored there."

"Good," David McCarter said. The Briton hated being unarmed. Without the familiar weight of a pistol in a shoulder holster under his arm he felt as awkward as if he was wetting his pants. "Were you able to get a Browning Hi-Power and an Ingram M-10?"

"I didn't have any luck getting the M-10," Vasquez answered. "Such weapons are very difficult to find in Mexico. A black-market source I know does a fair amount of trade with some South American countries. I got two Argentinean versions of the 9 mm Browning NATO M-1935. That is the pistol you wanted. Correct?"

"It'll do," McCarter said with a disappointed sigh.

"I also got some Brazilian versions of the Beretta M-92," Vasquez continued. "I understand you prefer 9 mm pistols and submachine guns. I was not able to get the Uzi requested, but I do have three Mendoza submachine guns in 9 mm parabellum and two American-made M-16 assault rifles. Sorry, but I couldn't manage the FAL rifle one of you seems to favor."

"I'll get over it," Gary Manning assured him. "What about explosives? Any luck getting some C-4?"

"Only three kilos," the Mexican replied. "Plastic explosives are difficult to get here. I was not able to get grenades or anything of that sort."

"I wonder if the terrorists have the same problem," Calvin James remarked. "Has there been any news about the 23rd SCL in the Yucatán?"

"Not to my knowledge," Vasquez answered, driving the station wagon from the lot onto the road leading to the exit. "Of course, I'm not actually part of any intelligence network. A lot of information doesn't filter through to free-lance operatives like me. I've heard there is supposed to be a terrorist training camp down there somewhere and supposedly the army has looked into it without finding any proof except for the bodies of an American schoolteacher and an old drunkard who was acting as his guide."

"Do you know who might be following us in the gray four-door?" Gary Manning inquired as he glanced out the rear window at the pursuing vehicle.

"Somebody tailing us?" Vasquez said with surprise. He looked in the rearview mirror. The dark gray sedan followed steadily behind them. "Are you sure the car is not simply going the same way?"

"I think it's a tail," McCarter commented in an annoyed tone. "Nondescript car, head count indicates three or four blokes inside, front license plate is smeared with mud or paint to make it difficult to read. They're staying about fifteen or twenty feet away, far enough to avoid direct suspicion, but close enough to follow us or even listen in with a rifle microphone. Hell, they might have even planted a mike in this station wagon while you were meeting us in the airport.''

''Oh, hell,'' Calvin James groaned. ''Sounds like CIA. The Company must have found out enough about our visit to get suspicious. Either that or they're keeping tabs on you for general purposes. This sucks. What are we going to do?''

''But they couldn't have known...'' Vasquez began lamely.

''You can't be sure of that,'' Katz told him. ''We can't be sure those men are CIA or any other intelligence outfit. Let's just see what happens farther down the road. In case they have a listening device in the car, cease all conversation.''

''A little late for that,'' McCarter muttered. ''If it is CIA or Mexican authorities, they've already heard enough to kill our mission before it begins.''

''I said cease conversation,'' Katz insisted in a firm voice.

Katz turned to the other members of Phoenix Force and tilted his head toward the pursuing car. Then he held up his prosthetic right hand and chopped the hard edge into the gloved palm of his left hand. The others nodded their understanding of his signal. Katz had warned them that there might be trouble and they had better prepare for it as best they could.

Gary Manning unsnapped the latch to his briefcase and opened the lid. Several metal pens were clipped to the curtain inside the lid. Some of the pens were exactly what they appeared to be. Others served a different purpose. The Canadian selected two of the gold pens with red bands at the middle. He slipped one into his breast pocket and the other into a side jacket pocket.

David McCarter unhooked the belt around his lean waist. He slid it through the belt loops of his trousers and pulled it free. The Briton removed his blazer before wrapping the belt around his waist without slipping it through the belt loops. The buckle was large, oval-shaped and made of black micarta treated with phenolic resins to harden it, and the rim of the buckle was stainless steel.

Calvin James carried a doctor's black satchel. His forged papers identified him as Ralph Brown, M.D., so he had no problem getting the bag through customs in the U.S. or Mexico. The labels on the vials in the satchel claimed the liquids and pills were simply penicillin, insulin and aspirins. Most of the labels were false.

The bag also included several syringes wrapped in plastic containers, cotton balls, a stethoscope, thermometer and a blood-pressure gauge with a mercury sphygmomanometer. James removed a leather packet from the bag and unzipped it. The packet contained some fundamental surgical instruments. He selected scalpels with the largest blades and carefully placed them in his breast pocket before closing the bag.

"What are you doing?" Vasquez inquired, trying to watch his passengers, the road and the rearview mirror all at the same time.

Katz placed his index finger to his lips to signal for silence. Vasquez sighed, shook his head slightly and continued to concentrate on his driving. The gray sedan still followed steadily behind the station wagon. The highway traffic near the airport was fairly heavy, and it seemed a safe bet for the Phoenix commandos that the tail probably would not try anything until they reached an area with less traffic and fewer witnesses.

Trucks, buses and automobiles zipped along the highway in large numbers, and a cloud of smog hovered above the buildings in the distance. Mexico City had the second largest population in the western hemisphere, second only to the New York metropolitan area. It had a lot of industries and a lot of motor vehicles that caused a serious air pollution problem. Phoenix Force's first view of Mexico City was less than appealing, but that was a secondary concern compared to the mysterious sedan following their vehicle.

Vasquez steered the station wagon into the right-hand lane as they approached the city. Katz noticed a battered old brown pickup truck parked at the side of the road with its hood raised. A man stood by the engine, and another one was positioned farther back. A pair of binoculars hung from his neck, and he held a walkie-talkie to his face, spoke into it and then tossed the radio into the back of the truck.

"Slow down," Katz told Vasquez. "You'll have to stop soon."

"*¿Que?*" the Mexican asked with surprise, confused by the Israeli's prediction.

The pickup truck suddenly pulled out from the side of the road and parked lengthwise in the path of the station wagon. Two men stood on the opposite side of the vehicle, Kalashnikovs in their fists. Vasquez stomped on the brake, and the wagon skidded to a halt less than a foot from the body of the truck. The sedan pulled up behind them and stopped.

The ambushers jumped out from behind the truck. Dressed in dirty chino pants, tattered field jackets and worn sneakers, both young men wore baseball caps and sunglasses and were also armed with AK-47s. A third figure, a young woman wearing the same type of apparel, appeared from the front of the truck. She held a revolver in a two-handed grip.

More figures emerged from the sedan. Two men charged forward with compact machine pistols in their fists. The men of Phoenix Force recognized the

guns. Czech-made Skorpion machine pistols, probably 7.65 mm or 9 mm caliber. The Skorpion was a
favorite of European terrorists. The nasty little
weapons were concealable, very destructive at close
range and easy to handle with minimum training.
The Red Brigade in Italy loved to use Skorpions to
"knee-cap" victims.

"I don't think these guys are CIA," James remarked, taking a scalpel from his pocket. He pressed
it into his palm, careful to keep the ultra-sharp blade
above the ridge at the base of his fingers.

"Get out!" one of the gunmen shouted as he
kicked the back fender and waved his Skorpion in a
threatening gesture. Another man repeated the command in Spanish.

"What should we do?" Vasquez asked fearfully.

"I think we should get out," Katz replied in a
voice that sounded far more calm than he felt under
the circumstances.

They opened the car doors and stepped outside
slowly. Katz and McCarter raised their hands to
shoulder level, and Manning and James held their
hands on top of their heads. Vasquez did not raise his
hands until one of the gunmen pointed an AK-47 directly at his face.

"What is the meaning of this?" Katz demanded,
his voice filled with indignation.

"Shut your mouth, you *gringo* pig," one of the rifle-toting ambushers snapped. "You are coming with us."

"I thought we came to Mexico City, not bloody Beirut," McCarter declared, folding his arms on his chest. "What the hell is this? A kidnapping?"

"What do you think these guys are doing?" James snorted. He and Manning faced the two gunmen with Skorpion blasters. "*¿Quién es usted? ¿Secuestradors? ¿Robachicos?*"

"So!" One of the Skorpion gunners smiled, revealing a gold tooth in the middle of his mouth. "The *negro yanqui* speaks some Spanish, eh? *Si*, this is a kidnapping, black one. You just shut your mouth and hope the government of *los Estados Unidos* will be willing to pay ransom for a boy like you."

"Ah sur'nuff hopes so," James replied in a sarcastic step 'n' fetch it imitation. His hands were still on top of his head with the scalpel hidden under his palms.

"Wait a minute," Manning began. His hands were also on top of his head and concealed one of his special pens. "I'm not a U.S. citizen. I'm a Canadian, damn it."

"Right," McCarter added, glaring at the two riflemen and the female terrorist with the revolver. "And I'm British. Take a look at my passport..."

"*¡Silencio, cochino!*" the woman hissed, and cocked the hammer of her revolver.

"All right," the Briton assured her. He thought that she was probably attractive when her dark features were not contorted with hatred. "No need to get nasty."

"Enough talk!" a rifleman snapped, then gestured with his Kalashnikov toward the truck. "Move! Now!"

"If you insist," Katz agreed as he lowered his right arm and pointed his prosthetic hand at the man's face.

The sharp crack of a high-velocity bullet breaking the sound barrier erupted, and a .22 Magnum slug smashed into the bridge of the terrorist's nose. He was dead before he could hear the shot that punched a hole though his brain. Perhaps he lived long enough to see orange flame burst from the end of Katz's index finger a fragment of a second before the bullet drilled into his skull.

The other terrorists were momentarily startled and confused. Smoke rose from the torn end of the gloved finger, which was actually the barrel of a pistol built into the prosthesis. They were unsure of what happened even when they saw the body of the slain gunman fall to the ground. The shot certainly distracted the remaining terrorists, and Phoenix Force immediately took advantage of the opportunity.

McCarter quickly unbuckled his belt. Without a jacket or belt loops to get in the way, the belt swung free as he held the leather in his fist and lashed out with the improvised weapon. The heavy buckle slashed into the face of the other rifleman. The terrorist's cheekbone split, and blood streamed down his face as he fell backward and triggered his AK-47.

The woman started to turn, undecided whether Katz or McCarter should be her target. Her comrade's Kalashnikov solved the problem for her. The man's weapon had shifted away from McCarter when the belt whipped into his face, and the barrel was pointed at the female terrorist when the gunman reflexively triggered his weapon. Three 7.62 mm rounds hit her between her firm young breasts. The woman's sternum exploded within her and bone fragments tore into vital organs. Her heart and lungs ravaged, she dropped her revolver and collapsed lifeless to the ground.

The rifleman tried to ignore the throbbing pain in the side of his face as he swung the AK-47 toward McCarter's position. The British ace had already rushed forward, the belt held between his fists. He raised his arms and used the belt like a leather bar to drive the barrel of the terrorist's weapon upward. The Kalashnikov spit out another salvo of bullets and fired the rounds harmlessly into the sky.

McCarter rammed a knee between his opponent's legs. The man groaned in agony as his testicles seemed to explode from the knee kick. Grabbing the rifle with both hands, McCarter wrenched it from the terrorist's grasp. The Briton turned slightly, the AK-47 in his left hand, and quickly smashed his right elbow into the point of his opponent's jaw. The terrorist staggered from the blow. McCarter whipped a backfist to the man's face and hammered a big knuckle right between his eyes. The terrorist uttered a soft moan and fell unconscious at McCarter's feet.

Katzenelenbogen scooped up the AK-47 dropped by the man he had shot, and McCarter also had the Kalashnikov he had taken from his opponent. They trained their rifles on the pickup truck as another terrorist leaned out the window on the driver's side and tried to point a sawed-off, double-barrel shotgun at the Phoenix pair.

The AK-47 rifles snarled with twin streams of 7.62 mm bullets. Some of the projectiles punched through the door of the truck and pierced the gunman's torso while other bullets ripped into his upper arms and face. The shotgun fell unfired from his trembling fingers, and he fell back across the front seat of the truck. The inside of the windshield and dashboard were splattered with the dead man's blood and brains.

Gary Manning and Calvin James had also gone into action the instant Katz fired his hidden .22. Manning had yanked both ends of the pen in his fists and snapped the band in the middle. The mercury fulminate fuse ignited as Manning hurled the pen to the ground near the feet of the two Skorpion submachine gunners. The magnesium flare within exploded, and a brilliant white light burst from the ground.

The glare blinded the two terrorists, but Manning and James were expecting it. The Canadian demolitions expert ducked low, lunged forward and raised a forearm under the frame of the closest opponent's Skorpion. The blow knocked the weapon upward as the half-blind terrorist triggered the Czech blaster. A volley of 7.65 mm rounds rattled away at the clouds.

Manning rammed a fist under the terrorist's ribs. The gunman groaned and started to double up from the sudden pain. Manning hammered his fist across his opponent's wrists and chopped the Skorpion from the man's grasp. The gun clattered to the ground.

The Canadian swung a left hook to the terrorist's jaw, making his head recoil from the powerful punch. Manning drove an uppercut to his opponent's solar plexus. The terrorist folded up from the blow as breath whooshed from his open mouth. For final effect Manning slammed a knee under the man's jaw. The hoodlum's teeth clashed together hard and his body slumped senseless to the ground.

Calvin James had also acted the instant the flare exploded. He had whipped his hand from the top of his head and hurled the scalpel at the snotty gunman with the gold tooth. The surgical instrument hit him in the upper right biceps. He cried out as the super-sharp steel bit into flesh and muscle. His arm jerked, and he pulled the trigger, but his aim had shifted from the violent spasm in his damaged limb.

Bullets hissed inches from James, close enough to send a shiver of terror up the black man's spine. But fear was part of the job, and he had been familiar with it since childhood. James did not freeze up from the near-brush with death. He bolted forward and swung a roundhouse kick to the triggerman's weapon. His foot booted the Skorpion out of the terrorist's hands, and he promptly lashed a cross-body karate chop across his opponent's face.

The blow immediately split the terrorist's upper lip. Copious blood flowed from his open mouth as he spit out his dislodged gold tooth. Seizing his opponent's shirtfront with his left hand, James withdrew the other scalpel from his pocket. He pulled the terrorist forward and slashed the steel edge across the side of the man's neck. The scalpel sliced deep, and blood squirted from a severed carotid artery. James immediately plunged the point of the scalpel into the hollow of the wounded man's neck.

James shoved the dying opponent to the ground. The terrorist thrashed about in the dust, clawing at the short handle of the scalpel buried in his neck. His struggles were brief because the blood loss and shock soon rendered him unconscious. Within moments he was dead. Calvin James wasn't paying any more attention to his opponent because he no longer had to worry about him. The black warrior took possession of the dead man's Skorpion. At least one opponent still remained in the sedan.

Manning had already gathered up the other Skorpion. The front door on the passenger's side popped open and a man emerged with an AK-47. Manning opened fire. Bullets hammered the car door without penetrating, but the window to the door was less durable. Two slugs shattered glass and drilled into the chest of the gunman. The terrorist groaned and stumbled away from the car, one hand clutched to his wounded torso while the other held the Kalashnikov and tried to fire the rifle. James triggered his Skorpion and got the gunman with a trio of bullets. The terrorist executed a final dive toward the ground.

Staring in horror from behind the windshield of the sedan, the last terrorist grabbed the steering wheel and shifted gears into reverse. Manning fired his Skorpion at the windshield as the guy stomped on the gas, and the windshield cracked crazily. The car shot backward as James added another wave of Skorpion slugs to the assault on the enemy sedan. He aimed low and blasted a salvo into the front tires and radiator. Air hissed from punctured rubber, and the car hood popped open, the latch broken. Water and steam poured from the ruptured radiator as the sedan rolled onto the highway.

It had moved directly into the path of a huge eighteen-wheeler that came bearing down like an unstoppable locomotive. The enormous truck hit the sedan broadside. The big grill and front fender tore through the crippled car as if it were made of plywood. The sedan burst apart, and chunks of it hurtled across the highway. If the driver had been alive, he certainly did not survive the collision. The eighteen-wheeler screeched to a halt. Traffic had come to an abrupt stop. Several fenders were bent and damaged, but the passersby were lucky and no one was injured by the sudden pileup.

"Come on, Vasquez," Katz urged as he pulled on the Mexican free-lance agent's arm. "We have to get out of here before the *federales* arrive."

"Ah . . . yes," Vasquez replied in a stunned voice. Everything had happened so fast he could not fully grasp it. Within a few seconds the four men had turned the tables on the terrorists. Bodies were everywhere and none belonged to the strange visitors he had met at the airport.

"Got two live ones," Manning declared as he dragged an unconscious terrorist to the station wagon. David McCarter hauled the other survivor to the car.

"Load them in, and we'll question them at the safehouse," Katz announced. The Israeli literally pushed Vasquez behind the steering wheel. "You do remember where that is, don't you?"

"*Si,*" Vasquez acknowledged with a nod as he started the engine. "But what was that all about?"

"We'll know more after we talk to these prisoners," Katz stated. He glanced in the back seat to be certain everyone was in the car. "Let's go."

The station wagon swerved onto the highway and headed up the only lane that was not blocked by stalled traffic. The vehicle raced from the scene of destruction and confusion. James and Manning tied the prisoners' wrist and ankles, using the captives' own belts and torn strips of clothing.

"Well," Manning commented with a shrug, "It didn't take us long to find some terrorists."

"Yeah," McCarter muttered sourly. "I can't believe how bleedin' lucky we can be at times."

7

Acapulco is one of the most popular tourist spots in Mexico. And little wonder, since it offers visitors visitors luxury hotels, flashy casinos and beaches rivaling the Riviera's. It is a perfect winter vacation area because the months of December, January, February and March are generally sunny and pleasant, although summer and autumn tend to be uncomfortably humid and frequently rainy.

It was early summer and the tourist trade was fairly low when Rafael Encizo, Manuel Cassias and Benito Tillo arrived at one of the small airfields outside Acapulco. Their pilot was a friend of Tillo's, a small-time smuggler who often assisted in the gunrunner's operations. Three other members of Tillo's personal syndicate also joined them for the trip from Tijuana to Acapulco.

The men had been introduced to Encizo only by their first names. The pilot was Armando, a tall, wiry man with a trimmed mustache and beard who seldom spoke and preferred to communicate with nods or shakes of his head. Another gunrunner pal of

Tillo's was Miguel, who was a big, muscular man. The third new member of Encizo's companions was Adolfo, small of stature and with a black patch over his left eye. The last addition to the group had the unlikely name of Fong. Part Chinese and part Mexican, Fong was originally from Mexicali where a small Chinese community had been formed by Asian immigrants who had headed south of the border from California after laboring on the railroad in the nineteenth century.

The group deplaned at the airfield and rented two Land Rovers available near the field. The canvas luggage loaded into the Rovers contained a variety of weapons. They were not headed for the luxury tourist digs in the heart of Acapulco. The city is located along the coast of the Mexican state of Guerrero. Deep-sea fishing, scuba diving and other watersports are very popular activities for tourists. Numerous fishing villages and boat-rental services line the coastal region near Acapulco.

Encizo was in his element because he had formerly worked as a scuba instructor at one of the boat-rental operations at a harbor near Acapulco. It was a beautiful area, with clear skies, generally clean water and excellent beaches. He had occasionally thought about returning to Acapulco for a holiday, but circumstances had brought him back to his favorite part of Mexico for a very different reason.

Tillo's men drove the Land Rovers along a little-traveled dirt road to an obscure fishing village about twenty kilometers south of Acapulco. Encizo had never been to the village before. It did not look like a regular tourist attraction. The mean-faced men standing outside the shanties did not look much like fishermen, either. Some wore straw sombreros and chinos, and others were in blue jeans or cutoffs. Most carried rifles or shotguns with belts of ammo strapped across their chests. A few had pistols holstered to their hips.

"Nice reception committee," Manuel Cassias remarked, and there was a slight quiver in his voice. He reached into his bag and withdrew his .357.

"Don't worry," Tillo assured him. "This is standard for the village when Montoya is here. These are some of his *bandidos*."

"For a moment I thought we'd entered a well-armed monastery," Encizo said dryly. He noticed that Tillo had made certain his Colt .45 was ready, so the gunrunner was not quite so sure there was nothing to worry about. "You say Montoya comes here often?"

"He likes to get away from the Yucatán," Tillo confirmed. "What better place than near Acapulco? He has some connections with pimps in the area. Helps them run their girls during the off season when the rich *yanquis* aren't here to spend money on *putas*."

"Sounds like a real entrepreneur," Encizo muttered as he took the Ruger P-85 from his bag and stuck it in the belt at the small of his back. "Adolfo, pass me the bag with the grenades."

"Grenades?" The one-eyed gunrunner was driving and could not turn to look at Encizo. "Why do you want the grenades?"

"Insurance," the Cuban answered. "Hurry up, I don't want the *bandidos* to take notice."

"I hope you know what you're doing," Tillo remarked as he passed the grenades to the back seat.

"I hope we *all* know what we're doing," Encizo replied, reaching inside the canvas sack.

A bandit whose shotgun was canted over his shoulder held up his hand to urge the two Land Rovers to stop. Three of his friends held rifles at port arms to reinforce the request. The first vehicle, driven by Miguel with Fong and Armando for passengers, came to a halt. Adolfo stepped on the brakes and followed suit.

"Buenos días, amigos," Tillo announced as he stood up to allow the bandits to clearly see him. "I want to talk to Francisco. Your *jefe* is expecting us."

"Sí, sí," a bandit said in a bored voice. "He told us he expected you, but he didn't say anything about these other *hombres*."

"We're going to talk to Montoya," Encizo stated as he stepped from the Land Rover with a grenade in one fist. He tossed a small metal object at the feet of the nearest *bandido*. "You know what that is?"

The man stared down at the small ring with a short stem. His eyes grew rounder when he recognized it as the pin of a hand grenade.

"Any of you shoot me, and my grip on this grenade will let up," Encizo announced, holding up his fist so the bandits could clearly see what was in his hand. "The spoon will pop off, and the grenade will explode in five seconds."

He grabbed the canvas sack with his other hand and jammed his fist into the mouth of the bag. "And I have nine more grenades in here," he announced. "Now, maybe you think you can run far enough to avoid getting blown to bits or you can reach into this bag and put the spoon and the pin back in the right grenade in less than five seconds."

"He's bluffing," a *bandido* stated, but he did not sound convinced of his own remark.

"I don't think he's bluffing," Tillo declared. He was nearly as surprised as the bandits by Encizo's actions. "I think maybe he's *loco* enough to do it."

"If we're going to see Montoya, you'd better get him soon," Encizo stated, meeting the hard gaze of the *bandidos* with his own unblinking stare. "My hand is starting to get tired."

The bandits seemed unsure of how to handle the situation. None of them put down their weapons, but none pointed their weapons at Encizo, either. Tillo,

Cassias and the others in Encizo's group were almost as nervous as the *bandidos*. The Cuban simply waited for the other side to make the next move. His expression revealed nothing. In fact Encizo's only thoughts were about finding his brother. If the bandits refused to help him, his goal would not be possible to accomplish. Encizo was not bluffing, and he was prepared to sacrifice his own life if necessary.

"Everyone calm down," a voice demanded from the doorway of a shack. "Just calm down."

A large man stepped from the threshold. A flabby beer belly hung over the gun belt around his thick waist, and his wide face was mostly concealed by shaggy black hair, a drooping mustache and an unkempt beard. He was dressed in a dirty undershirt, stained trousers and mud-splattered boots. The man folded his tattoo-covered arms on his chest and stared at Encizo.

"I am Montoya," he announced. "What do you want?"

"Alverez told me your people saw some terrorists led by Cuban soldiers in the Yucatán," Encizo answered. "I want to find them."

"Who is Alverez?" Montoya asked, then added, "Never mind. Put the pin back in the grenade and we'll talk."

"We're talking now," Encizo replied. "I don't have the pin anyway."

"Here it is, *señor*," a bandit said sheepishly, offering the grenade pin to Encizo.

"Hand it to one of my *amigos*," the Cuban told him. "I've got my hands full right now. I'll put the pin back in the grenade in a little while—that is, if any of us are still around."

"You brought a maniac with you, Benito," Montoya told Tillo. "I thought you less a fool than to play such games with me."

"I don't know this man very well," Tillo said with a trace of apology in his tone. "But what he has told me suggests his reason for seeking you concerns the best interests of both Mexico and *los Estados Unidos*."

"You may want to be a patriot," the bandit leader scoffed, "but it does not interest me, Benito. There is no profit in it."

"No profit in getting blown to bits, either," Encizo informed him. "But you can earn five thousand American dollars by helping me find the terrorists and the Cuban soldiers in the Yucatán."

"Death or five thousand dollars?" Montoya said with a shrug. "That's easy to choose. You got the money with you?"

"It's in Tijuana," Encizo answered. "You can send one of your *hombres* to get it."

"So you say," Montoya remarked doubtfully.

"He's telling the truth," Tillo assured him. "I give you my word as a matador it is true."

"Retired matador," Montoya commented.

"You question my word?" Tillo placed a hand on the grips of the Colt .45 thrust in his belt. "You doubt my honor?"

"No," the *bandido* boss insisted, aware that Tillo's machismo might trigger him into violence if he felt insulted. "I'll take your word about the money. Well, I wasn't in the Yucatán jungle to actually see the terrorists. Luis took the photographs. I suppose that's why you're here."

"Good guess," Encizo confirmed. "Is Luis here?"

"*Si, señor,*" a young bandit reluctantly admitted, and stepped forward. "I am Luis."

"Do you think you can find the location in the jungle where you came across the terrorists?" Encizo asked.

"Perhaps," Luis answered with a nervous nod. "But I can not be sure..."

"He'll find it," Montoya declared. "Take Luis with you. Let him be your guide in the Yucatán jungle."

"*Jefe...*" the young bandit began, his voice almost a plea.

"You do what I tell you," the *bandido* leader snapped. "This is business, Luis. You wouldn't be worth five thousand dollars if you lived to be a hundred. Not to me, anyway. You're not a very good thief, Luis. You got no *cojones*, either, so you're not that good in a fight. You're also illiterate and too stupid to ever become literate. Now I can make five thousand dollars by lending you to these *hombres*. I can also get rid of this *lunático* who threatens to blow us up. Those are some very good reasons to lend you to them, Luis. I can't think of a good reason not to. Can you?''

Luis lowered his head with shame and shook it slightly. He shuffled toward the Land Rovers and climbed into the back seat of the first vehicle. Luis sat beside Fong and handed his lever-action Marlin to the Chinese-Mexican. The young bandit looked as if he might start to cry.

"I keep my word, no?" Montoya stated. He smiled at Encizo. "Now, the money?"

"Give him the key, Manuel," Encizo told Cassias.

The smuggler stepped forward and handed a locker key to Montoya. "Send your man to the bus depot in Tijuana," Cassias explained. "The big one in the center of town. The locker number is on the key. There's an overnight bag in the locker with five thousand dollars in a plain brown envelope in the bag.''

"Gracias," Montoya grinned as he tossed the key into the air and caught it in his palm. He closed his fist around it and hastily pocketed the key. "Now, you get the hell out of here and take that *bastardo*

with the grenades with you. Don't ever let me see any
of your faces again. Especially you.''

The personal warning was directed to Encizo, but
the Cuban ignored the remark. He had not come to
Mexico to make friends, and he did not give a damn
what Montoya thought of him. He still held the bag
of grenades with his fist jammed inside as he backed
into the rear of the second Land Rover. Cassias and
Tillo climbed into the vehicle, and they took off
along the dirt road.

"Here's the pin," Tillo told Encizo in a sharp
voice. He handed the grenade pin to Encizo as they
sped away from the village. "Unless you still want to
get us all killed."

"It worked out all right," the Cuban replied as he
took the pin and inserted it into the grenade in his
fist. He put it into the bag with the others.

"You didn't tell me you were going to do anything like that stunt back there," the gunrunner
complained, jerking his head toward the village.
"That was unnecessary and dangerous. I know
Montoya. I could have gotten his cooperation without using such tactics."

"It's over now," Encizo told him. "May as well
drop it, Benito. We got what we came for, and that's
what matters."

"You cost me a connection with Montoya," Tillo
insisted. "He will never trust me again. That *bandido* knows other people I deal with. I can only guess

how many customers I have lost because of what you did back there."

"You've got other businesses," Encizo replied with a hard edge in his voice. "Legal businesses. Concentrate on them in the future."

"Rafael," Manuel Cassias began in a quiet voice, "what you did back there wasn't right. You took advantage of us, especially Benito. That was wrong."

"Maybe you're right, Manuel," Encizo was forced to admit. "I'm sorry, Benito. I had no right to risk your life and the lives of your men that way. That was stupid. It certainly won't encourage them to trust me in the future, will it?"

"I think we can survive the damage," Tillo said with a sigh.

"Most of all, I apologize to you, Manuel." The Cuban turned to Cassias. "You've already done so much for me and I repay you with treachery. I am sorry."

"No harm done, Rafael," Cassias replied, "but you aren't acting like yourself. I know you are desperate to find your brother, but this is becoming an obsession."

"Raul is the last remnant of my family," Encizo stated. "I have to find him. He is my flesh and blood, all that is left of my family. Can you understand that?"

"I understand," Cassias said with a nod, "but you must realize the odds of finding your brother are still quite low. He is, after all, a Cuban officer and a Communist. He's on the side of our enemies, Rafael. He'll regard you as an enemy, too."

"He's my brother," Encizo insisted.

"He's a stranger you haven't seen in nearly thirty years," Cassias told him. "Raul was a child then. He has grown into a man who has nothing in common with you. He's been educated and trained by the Communists."

"What would you do in my place, Manuel?" Encizo asked. "Forget I have a brother? Just leave him with the same regime that murdered our parents?"

"I don't know what I'd do," Cassias admitted. "I happen to know my brother, and I know where he lives in New Mexico. I haven't seen him in eight years, and I don't really care if I never see him again. Your brother might feel the same way. Blood might be thicker than water, but that doesn't always mean anything."

"You don't understand." The Cuban sighed. "I have to try. Raul is all the family I have."

"You still don't know him," Cassias insisted. "You have known me for years, yet you would have gotten yourself and us killed if Montoya hadn't cooperated. I think this thing about finding your brother is clouding your judgment. None of us can afford that, Rafael."

"I know," Encizo assured him. "I'm familiar with the rules. Make a mistake, and the price is your life and the lives of your teammates. That's how I've been living for some time. Somehow I thought this mission was different. Pretty stupid of me.''

"'Mission,' eh?" Cassias raised an eyebrow. "I'm rather curious about what sort of work you've been doing lately."

"You wouldn't believe it even if I could tell you," Encizo replied with a slight smile. He thought about his fellow Phoenix force members and wondered how they were doing without him. Maybe Brognola had already given them a new mission. He wondered if he would ever see any of them again.

8

"That's one of the things I hate about terrorists," Calvin James complained as he lowered himself into a battered old armchair and uttered a weary sigh. "They're such dumb bastards."

Ricardo Vasquez had taken them to his safehouse at the outskirts of Mexico City. It was an abandoned building, formerly a furniture storage house. They had parked the station wagon in a bay area and hauled the two prisoners into a small, cobweb-hung room for interrogation. James, Katzenelenbogen and Vasquez had conducted the interrogation, with James in charge of the administration of scopolamine and Katz supervising the questions for the captives.

Scopolamine is the only reliable truth serum. It is also a very powerful drug and potentially extremely dangerous. James had acquired considerable experience with using scopolamine since he had joined Phoenix Force. His medical background came in very useful at times, and handling scopolamine was a skill he had perfected over the years. None of his subjects had ever expired from a scopolamine injection, but he never took anything for granted while using the drug. James always examined a subject carefully to check for heart tremors, high blood pressure, evidence of diabetes, epilepsy and other physical conditions that would increase the risk of using the drug.

Katz's long experience in military and espionage operations of all sorts made him the best choice to supervise the interrogation. However, the Israeli's Spanish was less than fluent, and Vasquez had to translate. The interrogation had taken four hours. The two terrorists were in a scopolamine-induced trance that dulled their senses and left them only semiconscious. Questions had to be repeated to make certain they knew what they were being asked. Their speech was often slurred, not unlike a drunkard's, and difficult to understand. The prisoners also tried to resist the drug and lie while under the influence. The efforts always proved unsuccessful but were time-consuming. Eventually the terrorists' resistance broke down and they answered questions like obedient sleepwalkers.

"I hope you learned something from interrogating those two," Gary Manning remarked as he offered James a cup of black coffee.

"We learned that the terrorists tried to kidnap us only because they knew we arrived on a plane from the United States," Yakov Katzenelenbogen explained, lighting a cigarette. "They believed we really were just a group of Yardton Institute humanitarians."

"Hell, I figured out that much on my own," David McCarter snorted. The Briton had been busy inspecting the firearms Vasquez had acquired for Phoenix Force. He continued to load 9 mm cartridges into a magazine for a Mendoza subgun as he spoke. "They wouldn't have been so careless with us on the road if they suspected why we really came here. They probably would have just blown the station wagon to pieces with us in it. They could have hit us with a grenade or rocket launcher instead of trying to kidnap us."

"Deductive reasoning?" Manning stared at his British partner with surprise. "Don't tell me you're starting to use your head for something more than butting opponents in close-quarter combat."

"Bugger off," McCarter grunted, and displayed a two-finger salute. It was not a V-for-victory gesture.

"The important thing is we know for certain our cover hasn't been blown," Katz stated. "The terrorists simply practiced extraordinarily poor judgment in choosing us for a target."

"What reason did they have for jumping us?" Manning asked. "Did they intend to kidnap us for financial blackmail or political reasons?"

"Apparently both," Katz explained. "The two we captured are low-ranking members of the 23rd SCL, and neither of them is particularly bright. They didn't tell us much because they don't know much. However they did confirm that they received some training at a small base in the Yucatán run by some Cuban soldiers."

"Now we're getting somewhere," McCarter said cheerfully, but the expression on the faces of Katz, James and Vasquez were not encouraging. "Aren't we?"

"Not much," James said with a sigh. "I told you these dudes are dumb bastards. They know they were trained in the Yucatán, but they can't tell us anything else. They were taken to the jungle base in the back of a truck and couldn't see how they got to the location. They were transported from the jungle the same way, so all they could give us was a description of the jungle area. Ain't that great? All we have to do is go to the Yucatán and look through about eight hundred miles of jungle."

"One thing is encouraging," Katz stated. "They confirmed that the Cuban officers in charge of the base are Major Pescador and Captain Encizo. The captain is described as well-muscled, an expert in hand-to-hand and small arms, and he has a heart-shaped, strawberry-colored birthmark on his face. Definitely Rafael's brother."

"We know we're on the right track," Manning commented, pouring himself a cup of fresh coffee from an urn propped on a crate. "That terrorist attack was actually a stroke of luck."

"Not too impressive, considering it doesn't really help us," Vasquez muttered. He opened an ice chest and removed a chilled bottle of Dos Equis. "Where do we go from here?"

"Well," McCarter started, then paused as he approached the ice chest. He opened the lid and looked inside. The Briton frowned when he discovered Vasquez had only stocked beer in the container. "If the terrorists can't tell us how to find the base, I don't know who we're going to ask instead."

"Someone who would know about Cuban activities in Mexico," Katzenelenbogen answered with a shrug.

"Oh, hell," McCarter snorted. He turned to Vasquez. "I don't suppose you've got any Coca-Cola stashed around here someplace?"

"No," the Mexican cutout agent replied. "I thought beer and coffee would be enough. What's this about someone who would know about Cuban activities in Mexico? Are you planning to contact the CIA at the American Embassy?"

"That's not who I had in mind," Katz answered. "CIA isn't in a position to know details about Cuban clandestine operations. Frankly, the CIA has become hampered in its functioning everywhere. The

Company has trouble keeping secrets. Congressmen get access to top-secret information and go public with it, sometimes without any regard to national security. Investigative reporters, at least that's what they call themselves, write bestsellers about CIA operations and justify publishing classified material by saying 'the public has a right to know.' I don't object to the public knowing most of this material, but there's no way to inform the public without at the same time informing the enemies of the United States. Not surprisingly, the CIA is often reluctant or unable to act effectively abroad. Even more understandable is the reluctance of other intelligence outfits in other countries to cooperate with the CIA. After all, the security personnel in Western Europe or Japan or here in Mexico want to maintain their national security, and they're apt to see involvement with the CIA as jeopardizing their own security."

"That's a pretty harsh criticism," Vasquez said with a shrug. "Not without an amount of truth from what I've experienced during my time with the Company. But if we're not going to get help from the CIA, what do you have in mind? The *federales*?"

"Hardly," Gary Manning commented. He turned to Katz. "You're thinking of contacting the KGB, aren't you?"

"What?" Vasquez asked with astonishment plastered across his face. "You can't be serious."

"Of course I'm serious," Katz assured him. "The Soviet Union actually runs Cuba. Castro didn't send thousands of Cuban troops to Angola, Mozambique and other African nations just to give his men a change of scenery. Those soldiers are placed under the command of Soviet military advisers. The Soviets determine Cuban foreign policies on every level. The Cubans wouldn't be training terrorists here in Mexico without authorization from the Kremlin. In fact, the Soviets may have actually ordered it."

"Isn't that a rather extreme assumption?" Vasquez asked. "After all, the Soviets aren't responsible for all the world's ills."

"The Kremlin is behind a large portion of international terrorism," Gary Manning stated. "Directly or indirectly, the KGB influences, supports and manipulates terrorist groups all over the world. We've seen it too many times to deny that it goes on. And Mexico has been a hotbed of Soviet spy activity since the days of Stalin."

"You know where we can contact some KGB agents here in Mexico City, Ricardo?" McCarter inquired. "We'd like to have a chat with them."

"Wait a moment," Vasquez insisted. "You must know something about how espionage organizations operate. Maybe things are different in other parts of the world, but here we don't run around kidnapping and killing each other's agents. We generally allow them to operate freely and attempt to get information by observing them. That's what intelligence is, you know. Gathering information, not corpses."

"We don't want a bloodbath, my friend," Katz assured him. "But we don't have time for conventional intelligence methods, either."

"I know of several KGB agents operating from a main base at the Soviet Embassy," Vasquez admitted reluctantly. "Most of them are under CIA surveillance."

"We can get around that," Manning said with a nod.

"What about the two terrorists?" Vasquez asked. "Do you intend to kill them?"

"Whatever you might think about us, we really aren't murderers," Katz assured him. The one-armed Israeli slid his prosthesis into a shoulder holster rig and fitted the holster under his right armpit. He slipped his other arm through the leather harness as he continued, "Besides, I think we can still find a use for them."

He shoved a Beretta .92 autoloader into the leather sheath under his arm. The other three Phoenix Force pros had already donned shoulder rigs. James was also armed with a Beretta 9 mm compact, while McCarter and Manning carried NATO M-1935s. Vasquez gathered up his pistol, a U.S. military 45-caliber 1911-A1 Colt, a favorite sidearm of the Mexican armed forces.

"So where do we begin?" Vasquez asked, sliding the gun into a belt holster on his hip.

"You tell us," Katz replied. "We have to know who the KGB spies are and where to find them before we can make the next move."

"I was afraid you would say something like that," the Mexican said with a sigh.

9

Maria Santo tried to hold her camera steady as the jeep rolled and bounced over the crude dirt road. Captain Santiago glanced over his shoulder at the slim, youthful woman in the back of the vehicle. She was beautiful, with long black hair, an oval face, large dark eyes and full lips. Her figure was quite fetching although she wore a bush shirt, jeans and boots. Santiago thought women should be required to wear dresses at all times. Women in men's clothing was how all this nonsense about women being equal to men got started, the captain thought sourly.

Of course, Santiago would have objected to a civilian passenger with a military truck convoy regardless of the individual's sex or reason for being present for such an operation. A female newspaper reporter would have been Santiago's last choice for company on such a venture. The world was truly insane when such things could be ordered of an officer in the Mexican National Army.

It was politics, the captain realized. The civilian government was trying to show its population how civil its military had become. Probably more to please the *gringos* up north then the people of Mexico. Public relations and social reforms, Santiago thought sourly. A major national newspaper had sent a team of reporters to the army base along the Yucatán border. They were writing a story about how the military functioned in the jungle region. How they trained for combat, prepared for natural disasters and basic operations on a daily level. If people are that curious about the military, Santiago thought, they ought to join the army and find out for themselves.

However, the colonel had allowed the reporters on base, and they had interviewed soldiers, poked around in the motor pool, commo sections and various orderly rooms, and even eaten in the mess hall. Then the reporters wanted to go into the field with the troops. The colonel refused permission for the female reporter to go to the firing range or tank maneuver exercises. At least there was some indication of keeping the woman in her place, Santiago thought with a glimmer of satisfaction.

The captain just wished he had not been saddled with the Santo woman. She had complained about being left at the base while her male counterparts got to cover the action in the field. The colonel decided to get Santiago's company to keep her busy. Santiago figured she might be bad for the general morale of the men, so he decided to send her with the convoy just to get her off the base. He quickly regretted the notion when the colonel informed him it was his responsibility to personally look after the woman's safety. So Santiago took charge of the convoy and even allowed the reporter to accompany him in the lead vehicle.

The convoy was not sent on a dangerous mission. Three trucks hauled office equipment, field rations and machine parts in need of repair. Every other month, broken machinery that could not be fixed by personnel at the base was rounded up and taken to a repair center near Merida, the capital of the Yucatán state. Ordinarily Santiago would not think of wasting his own precious time on such a mundane assignment, but the woman's presence changed everything. A simple supply section duty that could have been trusted to an NCO now required the captain as chaperon. He did not trust the reporter alone with the troops. She might ask embarrassing questions about how things are done on an army base, and the youthful soldiers would be inclined to talk too much to a lovely woman with a friendly smile and a gentle voice.

The trip was visually pleasant. A cool breeze from the gulf to the north compensated for the hot noonday sun. The moderate climate allowed them to enjoy the lush growth of tropical trees, riot of multicolored flowers and exotic birds inhabiting the region. The road was located along the edge of the jungle, close enough to offer a clear view of the scenery, yet far enough to avoid running into a jaguar. There were still some of the big spotted cats in the Yucatán region, or so Santiago had heard. He had never personally seen a jaguar roaming free, and he certainly did not want to encounter one while the Santo woman was among them.

"There is talk about cutting down more and more of the forests in this area," Maria stated as she lowered her camera. "It would be a pity to lose all this natural beauty, don't you think?"

"I am a soldier not a conservationist," Santiago replied gruffly. Actually he agreed with her, but he was not sure what the military view on the subject was supposed to be. "I leave such matters in the hands of people who know more about it than I do."

"If you say so, Captain," she said with a shrug, aware of Santiago's resentment and his unwillingness to talk about virtually everything.

"Capitán," the jeep driver began in a bid for attention, then pointed at a group of figures dressed in dirty white cotton and straw sombreros. The *peónes* were clustered in the road, most kneeling next to the prone figure of a companion. One man seemed to be waving at the convoy to come forward. "It looks like an accident."

"Sí," Santiago agreed. "They appear to have an injured man. We'll stop and see if they need help."

The jeep came to a halt roughly three meters from the group. The trucks in the convoy followed the example of the lead vehicle and stopped behind the jeep. Santiago and a senior NCO from one of the trucks climbed out and prepared to investigate the accident. Maria started to step from the jeep, but Santiago shook his head.

"Wait here until we know what's going on," the captain told her. "This may be nothing, but we may have to get medical assistance for one of the *peónes.*"

"Perhaps I can help," Maria began.

"It is best you stay here," Santiago insisted. "I recall seeing an injured farmer on a road such as this. He had been gored by one of his own cattle. The horn had gouged him in the lower abdomen. His trousers were open and his genitals exposed, as well as some of his intestines. I doubt he would have wanted a woman to see him in that condition and he would not have wanted his picture taken at that moment, either."

"I wasn't thinking of a subfeature for my story," Maria told him, offended by the implication.

"Then allow these people some privacy," Santiago said sharply. "It would be a refreshing change if you newspaper people granted *someone* some privacy."

He turned on his heel and started to walk toward the *peónes.* The NCO had already approached the group. He stopped abruptly when two of the peas-

ant farmers raised their cotton shirts and withdrew
blue-black pistols from the waistbands of their trousers. The sergeant opened his mouth to shout a
warning to the others. The pistols snarled in unison,
and two slugs smashed into the chest of the NCO
before he could utter a sound. His punctured heart
stopped pumping blood, and he fell to the ground,
already more dead than alive.

The other *peónes* drew handguns. The man on the
ground rolled over, a Skorpion machine pistol in his
fists, the muzzle pointed at the convoy. Guns roared
and bullets split the windshield of the jeep. Holes
appeared in the thick glass screen, and a spiderweb
of cracks covered the surface. The driver slumped
back in his seat, his face destroyed by bullets and
shards of glass.

Maria jumped from the jeep. Santiago swept out
his left arm and pushed her to the ground as his right
hand clawed at the button-flap holster on his hip.
Maria saw torn fabric in the captain's shirt at the
ribcage. Blood oozed from the bullet wound, but
Santiago still drew his pistol, and working the slide
to his Colt .45, chambered the first cartridge and
aimed at the ambushers.

An enemy Makarov fired and pumped a slug into
Santiago's upper torso. The bullet split his sternum,
but he managed to trigger his Colt before he started
to fall. A terrorist cried out and tumbled backward
even before Santiago hit the ground. The force of the

big .45 projectile to the chest immediately took the gunman out of the game.

Automatic rifles erupted from the trees. Windows and windshields burst from the trucks. Drivers and soldiers inside the cabs collapsed with deadly wounds in their chests and heads. Two soldiers managed to jump out of the vehicles only to be ripped open by the salvo of full-auto rounds that assaulted the convoy from all four sides.

Maria lay sprawled on the ground and covered her head, the camera forgotten beside her. Her heart raced wildly, and she trembled with fear. She dared not raise her head because a bullet might crash into her face just the way the driver of the jeep had been killed. Maria did not want to witness the carnage all around her, yet she slowly uncovered her head and opened her eyes.

Santiago was kneeling on the ground near her. Remarkably the captain was still alive and conscious. There was a crimson flow from his bullet-torn chest, yet he still held his Colt and aimed it at the opponents in the road. The big .45 bellowed and another terrorist doubled up with a long moan. The sombrero fell from the wounded man's bowed head. He clutched his belly with both hands and wilted to the ground, his stomach a bleeding mass of ruptured tissue.

The gunman with the Skorpion trained his Czech machine pistol on Captain Santiago and opened fire.

Five 7.65 mm rounds tore into the soldier's chest and face. He tumbled backward and rolled across Maria's legs. She gasped but restrained a scream when she felt Santiago's body twitch for the last time. Blood seeped through her right pant leg. The warm dampness touched her thigh, yet she remained still on the ground. Maybe she could play dead long enough for the ambushers to be convinced that the massacre was complete.

"That was easier than shooting crippled ducks in a public fountain," she heard somebody announce with a chuckle. The man's tone suggested he might be speaking from personal experience. "We chopped those fascist pigs to pieces!"

The other terrorists looked over at Pedro Garcia. The big 23rd SCL flunky seemed delighted with the victory as he marched from the treeline with a Kalashnikov canted on his brawny shoulder. Several other SCL gunmen accompanied Garcia, and they laughed and bragged as they strolled toward the convoy. Those among the terrorists who had been disguised as *peónes* did not find the moment as joyous as those who had fired on the soldiers from the cover of the trees. One of their companions lay dead and another was seriously wounded. The realities of battle were far more apparent to the survivors of the smaller group of men.

Captain Raul Encizo led the rest of the attack force from the opposite side of the rain forest. The

Cuban had commanded the attack. It was supposed to have been a simple ambush, and there had been little doubt it would be a one-sided confrontation. But they had not expected any of the soldiers to be armed. Apparently only one officer in the convoy had carried a side arm, yet he had still managed to take out two of the SCL terrorists during the gun battle. Captain Encizo was less than pleased with the performance of the terrorists thus far. He was unhappy with himself, as well, since he had helped train the SCL units.

The previous day a group of terrorists had attempted to kidnap some American busybodies from the Yardton Institute. That should have been child's play even for amateurs, but something went wrong. Very wrong. Captain Encizo and Major Pescador had not been able to learn the details about the ambush on the highway in Mexico City; however, they learned that all but two of the terrorists involved had been killed. The pair that were not corpses on the highway had vanished along with the Yardton Institute eggheads—if they really were what they had claimed to be.

Since the first terrorist operation had failed so totally and unexpectedly, Encizo personally took charge of the attack on the truck convoy. The mission, especially when compared to the earlier operation, had been a success, but it had not gone as smoothly as he had hoped. He saw Garcia approach the wounded terrorist and kneel beside the man, then glance up at the others and shake his head solemnly. Captain Encizo did not have much respect for Garcia, but he guessed the muscular terrorist was correct about the condition of the wounded man.

Garcia slowly drew a pistol from his belt and stuck the muzzle under the jaw of the injured terrorist. Most of the others looked away. At least two of them crossed themselves. The Communist doctrine endorsed by the terrorists had not canceled out all of their Catholic upbringing, Encizo noticed. Garcia triggered his pistol, and the roar of the gunshot announced the end of the unlucky terrorist's life.

"Was this necessary, *Capitán*?" another SCL member asked Encizo. Garcia had shot the wounded man, but the Cuban had not tried to stop him. That was the same as approving the action.

"He would have died within an hour or so," Encizo replied. "Would you rather die quickly or slowly with much agony?"

Several terrorists had moved to the trucks. They chattered away in excited voices as they climbed into the back of each vehicle, but the cargo disappointed them. They had hoped to find weapons, medical supplies, food or something useful. Broken machinery was worthless to the jungle-based terrorists.

Others opened the doors to the cabs of the trucks and started to haul out some of the bodies of the slain drivers and passengers. One man was still alive.

His right shoulder had been shattered by rifle bullets and his face badly cut by flying glass, but he was still alive and semiconscious. The terrorists cheered with sadistic anticipation as they dragged the soldier from the vehicle.

"No!" he croaked weakly as he saw two terrorists draw knives. *"¡Por favor!"*

A knife-wielding terrorist spat out a vicious curse and grabbed the wounded soldier's hair with one fist while the other lowered the blade to his face.

Maria heard the soldier's terrible scream. Not knowing what they were doing to the poor trooper, she lay motionless on the ground, praying that the nightmare would end and thinking that she would almost welcome death if it would stop the horror. A pair of boots stamped the ground beside her. Maria held her breath and wanted to stop her heart from beating so fast. The pulse behind her ear sounded like a drum. It hammered at her skull so loudly she was certain the terrorist would hear it.

Raul Encizo stepped over the woman's body and marched toward the terrorists who were busy torturing the wounded soldier. They had already cut off the man's ears and nose. One of the sadists was about to poke his blade into an eye when Encizo grabbed the terrorist's collar and yanked him backward, dumping the man onto the ground. The others stepped back as Encizo pointed his AK-47 at the mutilated face of the tortured soldier.

He fired a single round into the forehead. The terrorists grumbled with disappointment that their cruel sport had been terminated so suddenly, but Encizo shook his head with disgust. Combat was something he understood. The Cuban believed there was nothing more noble than a battlefield. Fighting a man face-to-face was more than a test of skill and courage: it was also a duel of philosophies and politics with the words stripped away. But torture was a foul perversion of combat, a sport for cowards and bullies.

"We have no time to waste on this nonsense," the captain informed his troops. "You are soldiers for the revolution of the oppressed masses, not bandit butchers."

"Whatever you say, *Capitán*," Garcia remarked as he gathered up the camera. He looked down at the woman's body and frowned. "I wonder what she was doing with these soldiers? This must have belonged to her."

"The woman was probably a pawn of the capitalists," Captain Encizo said with a shrug as he took the camera from Garcia. "She must have been part of some sort of propaganda campaign to try to convince the people of Mexico that the present federal republic is a better political system than true communism. It is sad that women are used by the imperialists in this manner. Only in a true Communist state can women ever be equal to men."

"Oh, really?" Garcia laughed. "The British and the Israelis have elected women as prime ministers. The *norteamericanos* have women in congress, as governors, and placed in cabinet positions in the federal government. Odd, but I don't recall any women in any Communist country with a position of authority except Milka Planinc in Yugoslavia. But you Cubans and the Soviets don't really approve of Yugoslavia's brand of communism. Do you?"

" 'True equality under communism can only exist when all capitalism is crushed and people can unite worldwide under a single pure socialist government which will redistribute wealth equally among all people and end positions of rank and authority,' " Encizo replied, quoting the Party line.

Garcia nearly laughed in his face. Was this parroting, brainwashed Cuban tin soldier serious? Did he really believe Castro would give up his office or everyone in the Soviet Union would be able to drive big Russian Zims like the hotshots in the Kremlin? Or did he believe the Party leaders would scrap their automobiles and take the train like the other citizens? Utopian stupidity. Yet Garcia realized he had already criticized enough to upset Encizo. It would be dangerous to anger the Cuban with more offensive remarks about the perfect world he believed could one day be created by violence, revolution and lies.

"That may be, *Capitán*," the terrorist stated. "Personally, I don't really want women to be equal to men anyway. Too bad this one is dead. She was a beauty. We could have had a bit of fun with her before executing her..."

"No man under my command will rape a woman under any circumstances," Captain Encizo said sharply. "Too many of you 23rd SCL revolutionaries still think like barbarian trash. I will not tolerate such behavior. It is an offense to the purpose of the revolution."

"So it is all right if we kill an unarmed woman as long as we don't screw her first?" Garcia snorted with disgust.

Frustrated, the terrorist kicked the woman's body. Maria's body stiffened from the sharp pain in her ribs. She bit her tongue and stifled a groan. Tears seeped between her eyelashes, but she did not utter a sound or move. *Madre de Dios,* she thought desperately, *please don't let him kick me again.*

"That's it," Captain Encizo said as if answering Maria's prayer. "We're finished here. It is time to leave."

"What about the trucks?" a terrorist asked.

"They are no use to us in the jungle," the Cuban replied gruffly. "Bring the bodies of our dead and leave the rest. We've been here long enough, and there is much more work to be done."

10

A vicious-looking insect with mean pincers crawled over Maria's right hand. Spindly legs tapped along her flesh to the knuckles in an eager rush for prey. The creature was a hunter, and it sensed prey nearby, yet it could not locate the target.

Maria Santo still lay sprawled on the ground next to the corpse of Captain Santiago. She barely noticed the creeping tiny feet on the back of her hand. Numerous insects had descended upon the scene of the massacre. Her eyes were closed, but she heard the maddening buzzing of hundreds of flies that hovered around the lifeless bodies of the slain soldiers. Scavenger beetles had also been drawn to the piles of dead flesh. She felt them crawl over her prone figure, but she did not stir.

The terrorists had left. Maria did not know how much time had lapsed since she had been pushed to the ground by Santiago. Perhaps it had been mere minutes or hours or even days. To her it seemed an eternity had passed while she lay on the ground and pretended to be dead, and lying like that had come to feel almost natural. There was little reason to get up or even open her eyes. She knew what she would see—the corpse of Santiago and the bodies of his men. She did not want to see that, and she did not want to chance discovering that one or more of the murderers had stayed behind.

Maria had no idea what she would do if she did shake off the numbing effects of the emotional trauma and rise from the ground. She was not sure where she was or which direction to head for to seek safety. The terrorists were out there somewhere. What way led to safety rather than to the lair of the murderous brutes who had ambushed the convoy? The thought started to whir in her head. Why had they done it? There was no logical reason to attack a group of trucks carrying old equipment to be repaired. Were they madmen? No. Madmen do not organize and attack random targets.

Perhaps it had not happened, Maria thought, finding comfort in the notion. The whole terrible incident could just be a dream. Maybe she was still asleep in her apartment in Mexico City, and she would wake up to find the alarm-clock radio blaring mariachi music. Carlos might even be in the bed beside her. Maria's fiancé was an airline pilot, and he was gone on a flight to Europe, but that might be part of the dream....

The raucous call of a bird finally penetrated her senses, and Maria opened her eyes. She crawled away from the corpse of Captain Santiago and clambered stiffly to her feet, but kept her head turned away from the convoy to avoid looking at the bodies. The air seemed to stink of decay and death. Shadows passed through the sky above, and she glanced up to see several vultures patrolling the sky in graceful circles, waiting to be certain everything below was dead before descending.

"It's not a dream," Maria told herself. She took a deep breath and winced from the pain in her ribs. "Uhh. That *bastardo* really kicked me, and these soldiers are really dead . . ."

Finally her gaze was drawn to the bodies. The corpses were sprawled beside the trucks, and she could see flies feasting on the open wounds. She looked away again and tried to think of what to do. Judging from the position of the sun low in the west, it would be dark in another hour or two. She did not relish the idea of walking back to the base at night. Snakes, jaguars, and God knew what else might be lurking in the forest, but none of the animals inhabiting the jungle frightened her as badly as the possibility of encountering the terrorists again.

Maybe the best thing was to simply stay put, she thought. The colonel would certainly wonder what had happened to the convoy and would surely send out search parties. The problem with that plan was she would have to stay with the trucks and the grisly collection of corpses that would attract more—and bigger—scavengers.

Her only other choice was to try to drive one of the army vehicles. Maria did not want to get inside the trucks or the jeep and sit in a pool of blood. She did not want to use a steering wheel splattered with brains or have slivers of bone on the seat next to her.

But she did not want to die, either.

Maria walked to the jeep. Her legs felt weak, and her head started to spin, making her stomach turn as she approached the first vehicle. The driver's corpse was still wedged behind the shattered windshield, his face a crimson pulp covered with flies. A few shards of glass jutted from the bloodied mess and twinkled obscenely in the fading sunlight.

For a few moments she thought she might pass out, but then forced herself to think of the dangers and started to prepare to pull the dead man from the jeep. Before her trembling fingers could touch the corpse, Maria noticed the steam hissing from the front of the vehicle. She moved closer to the hood and saw water and steam spitting from the nose of the vehicle.

She glanced down at the ground and discovered a pool of muddy water under the jeep. The radiator had been punctured by several rifle rounds. There might be enough water left to drive the jeep a kilometer or so, but it would not go much farther than that. She was almost relieved that she would not have to move the corpse from behind the steering wheel, but she still had no means of leaving.

Maria moved to the truck at the rear of the convoy. She had to step over three mangled-looking corpses to get there, but the trip proved unnecessary and bitterly disappointing. The gas tank had been ruptured and the fuel had poured out. Two tires had also been punctured by bullets. The remaining trucks were trapped between the two disabled vehicles. Bowing her head, Maria wiped her eyes with the back of her hand. She did not want to cry. The fear, frustration and sheer horror of the situation was mounting up inside her, but somehow she would survive.

A sudden ray of hope made her search the vehicles for a two-way radio. Only the jeep was equipped with a small field radio, and it had been smashed during the ambush. Maria threw the radio to the ground in frustration. She backed away from the scene of carnage to find a clearing where she could sit down and think without breathing the stench of death.

"Think, Maria," she told herself. "You've got to keep your wits and think this through. The colonel will send someone to find you. His men are probably already looking by now. You've got to stay put and wait."

Some of the vultures had landed near the corpses. Their big black wings flapped, and they shrieked at one another in a threatening manner. The dispute was brief, and soon each bird staked out part of a corpse, jealously guarding its claim from the others. Maria turned away, not wishing to see what would happen next.

She closed her eyes, and her imagination plastered across her mind's eye a vivid mental display of what the vultures would do to the dead soldiers. The sound of sharp beaks and talons tearing flesh mingled with the cries of the scavenger birds. Maria hugged her belly. She knew she was going to be ill.

Maria was right.

11

Colonel Nikita Ivanovich Kalinin hated Mexico City. It was too crowded, too noisy and too full of a Latin American culture that was as much Indian and *yanqui* as Spanish. Formerly Kalinin had been stationed at the Soviet Embassy in Madrid. Spain was a bit backward, in Kalinin's opinion, but at least the Spanish knew they were Spanish. He had been in Mexico for two years and still could not begin to understand its people.

Kalinin wished he had mastered a different language instead of Spanish. French may have been a better choice, he suspected. It would not be so bad to be stationed in Paris. Of course, he had never had much say about such decisions. The Soviet state-run schools determined one's education goals at an early age. Kalinin scored high on IQ tests, and he was determined to have the chance to learn a foreign language. In the fifties, the Soviets were still trying to establish a stronghold of communism in Central and South America. For whatever reason, Kalinin was chosen to master Spanish.

While an officer in the Soviet Army, Kalinin was recruited by the GRU—military intelligence—and spent three years in Africa as an adviser. His main duties consisted of supervising Cuban troops, first in the People's Republic of the Congo and later in Angola in the late 1970s. Kalinin hated Africa. The climate was hot all year round. Like most Soviets, he felt a great love for his homeland and missed the change of seasons. He would welcome a freezing cold snowstorm if it was in Moscow or Leningrad. He had hoped to spend a few years in his own country after he returned from duty in Africa, but fate had other plans for him.

He was recruited from the GRU and transferred to the KGB, the Committee for State Security and the largest and most powerful intelligence network in the world. The KGB was impressed by Kalinin's record and even allowed him to keep the rank of senior captain he earned while with the GRU. The KGB also had a new post for Kalinin in Madrid.

Following the death of his control officer in Spain, Kalinin was promoted to major and placed in charge of KGB operations in the Madrid region until 1985. He was ordered back to Moscow, spent less than a year in Mother Russia and then he was sent to the Soviet Embassy in Mexico City. The appointment included another promotion to the rank of lieutenant colonel. Kalinin's career was technically successful, but he had found little satisfaction or pleasure in his job. All he really wanted to do was return to Russia and spend the rest of his life in his own country. Yet, as long as the KGB had use for him elsewhere, Kalinin would not be going home.

Colonel Kalinin sat in the back of a black Oldsmobile as the long car worked its way through the heavy downtown traffic in Mexico City. It was a nice car. Kalinin had not had much association with Americans. The Kremlin claimed they were Russia's worst enemies, but Kalinin remembered when the Chinese and the Albanians were supposed to be Russia's greatest allies. The colonel was basically indifferent toward Americans, but he did like their cars.

"Eto spravah, Mikhail," Kalinin instructed the driver, and as he leaned forward, he caught the worried expression on the face of the man sitting beside him.

"Da, Tovarisch," Mikhail replied with a nod, and steered the car into the left lane as ordered.

"I'm a bit concerned about this meeting, Comrade Colonel," Captain Aleksandr Reutov confessed. "Sarkisov's cover hasn't been secure for more than a month. This could be a trap by the CIA."

"Extremely unlikely," Kalinin replied, slightly amused by Reutov's paranoia about the American intelligence network. The CIA was only a fraction of the size of the KGB, and it had its figurative hands full with Nicaragua and Iran, not to mention problems within the Company itself and the Congress of the United States.

"Not that unlikely, Colonel," Reutov insisted. "Sarkisov was under surveillance by the CIA. They suspect he's one of your people, Colonel...."

"They discontinued surveillance two weeks ago," the colonel said with a sigh. "Whatever they suspected about Sarkisov, it didn't convince them he was worth putting time and effort into watching him. Sarkisov is a minor level agent. He's not really worth much effort by the CIA."

"But he's obviously learned something very important or we would not be rushing to this clandestine meeting," Reutov commented. "Correct, Comrade Colonel?"

Kalinin simply shrugged. Sarkisov was a bottom rung on the KGB ladder in Mexico City. He was not even an undercover agent, let alone a "sleeper." Sarkisov's cover was as a research assistant and translator for a noted archaeologist from the Soviet Union who was studying the ancient Mayan ruins. That cover offered Sarkisov ample opportunities to scan through dozens of libraries and obtain lots of overt intelligence. Nonclassified information was readily available and perfectly legal to collect through sources that were not labeled "confidential," let alone "top secret." Surprisingly, considerable amounts of valuable information about a nation's government and military can be learned by overt sources.

The CIA's suspicions about Sarkisov had been predictable, but the "researcher" was not doing anything illegal even if he was working for the KGB. In fact American journalists did exactly the same thing without working for any sort of intelligence network. However, it was possible Sarkisov may have come across something unusual. His phone call to Kalinin suggested that. Sarkisov had given him a brief message with passwords previously established by Kalinin to tell the colonel he needed to meet him and where without tipping off anyone who might have the phone tapped. It was the first time Sarkisov had used that emergency system, and the matter might prove important indeed.

Not that Kalinin had much reason for concern. He, Reutov and Mikhail all had diplomatic immunity. They could get away with almost anything without having to worry about the authorities. Unless they could be proved guilty of subversive espionage or a serious crime such as murder, neither the Mexican security forces nor the CIA could touch them. Even then it was more likely they would be deported than arrested, although being sent back to the U.S.S.R. under such conditions would probably mean disgrace, a quiet trial and either a sentence to a Siberian labor camp or a firing squad.

Kalinin glanced out the window at the blur of lights. At night Mexico City reminded him more of Rome than Madrid. A modern city with frantic traffic and busy nightlife. It was difficult to think that it had been victimized by one of the worst earthquakes in the last decade. Kalinin had arrived shortly after the quake two years before. He remembered the piles of rubble, the homeless people in the streets, the wounded being tended by Red Cross personnel and the *federales* guarding the wrecked property from bands of looters. It had been a terrible ordeal for Mexico City, but the people dealt with it with dignity and courage. Kalinin did not care much for Mexico or its people, yet he admired their strength in a crisis.

At last Mikhail parked the Olds in an alley next to a small restaurant that had been closed for nearly two months. Although technically out of business, the place was not on the market for sale. It actually belonged to a Mexican double agent working for the KGB. A light was on in a window. Kalinin and Reutov emerged from the car and walked to the side door. Reutov pulled back his jacket and placed a hand on the butt of the Makarov pistol holstered under his arm.

Kalinin took a key from his pocket and unlocked the door. The KGB agents entered the dining room. Chairs and tables were covered with white cloth shrouds although there was little dust because a cleaning company was contracted to see to the general upkeep of the place regularly.

The dining room was dark except for one light near the drawn curtains at the side window and another above the door. The two KGB agents had stepped into a spotlight and shadows surrounded them. Kalinin began to fear that Reutov's concern about a trap might be right after all.

A greeting came from the shadows as a shape rose from a table near the agents. The voice continued in Russian, "Please have a seat."

Reutov gripped his Makarov and drew it from leather. A metal click drew his attention to a tall, lean figure that materialized from the gloom and pointed a pistol at Reutov's head.

"Nyet," the man ordered, gesturing with his other hand to urge the KGB officers to raise their arms.

"Don't argue with my associates," Yakov Katzenelenbogen explained as he moved from the table. "They don't speak Russian anyway so it won't do you any good."

David McCarter emerged into the light, his Browning pistol still pointed at Reutov's head. He carefully plucked the Makarov from the captain's hand, then expertly frisked both men. Reutov had a diminutive 6 mm autoloader in an ankle holster for backup. Kalinin was unarmed.

"Easy on my suit, asshole," Kalinin declared in English, doing his best to sound like an American.

McCarter responded in French spoken with a proper Parisian accent. He poked Kalinin in the back with his pistol, and Katz ordered him sharply to stop. They were maintaining a pretense of French for the benefit of the KGB men.

"Oui," McCarter replied, and walked backward to Katz, Browning still pointed at the two KGB agents. He handed Reutov's pistols to Katz.

The Israeli placed the guns on a table. "Don't do anything to aggravate or confuse Marcel. He's very fond of shooting people. There's no need for anyone to get hurt unless you do something stupid."

Calvin James and Gary Manning stepped through the doorway. They dragged Mikhail's limp body with them. The black commando drew a Beretta from his belt and covered the KGB agents while his Canadian partner lowered Mikhail to the floor. Kalinin noticed Mikhail was still breathing. He was unconscious, not dead.

"Who is this?" Katz asked, glancing down at Mikhail. Katz nodded approvingly when informed that the unconscious man was the chauffeur. Then he switched back to Russian. "Now, Colonel Kalinin, let's talk."

"Who are you people?" Kalinin asked. "Sûreté?"

"No," Katz assured him, taking out a pack of French cigarettes purchased at a local tobacco shop for the occasion. "My associates are contract personnel from the Caribbean. Best we could come up with on short notice.''

"Guadeloupe or Martinique?" Kalinin inquired.

"Does it matter?" the Israeli said with a shrug. He offered the cigarettes to the KGB officers. Reutov declined, but Kalinin took one.

"Spacibo," the colonel thanked Katz as the Phoenix commander held a lighter to his cigarette. "And who are you working for?"

"That isn't important, either," Katz told him, taking a cigarette for himself. "What is important is the location of the 23rd SCL terrorist training camp headed by a Major Pescador of the Cuban army. Probably military intelligence."

"I don't know what you're talking about," Kalinin replied with mock astonishment. "I'm with the security staff at the Soviet Embassy. I have diplomatic immunity..."

"No one is immune to a bullet in the head," Katz told him. "We're not interested in political channels or playing typical espionage games with the KGB. Do you know how we got Sarkisov to call you? We injected him with truth serum and held a telephone to his head. The poor fellow is in the kitchen sleeping off the effects of scopolamine. There are also two Mexican terrorists in there taking a nap. The KGB can do whatever they want with those two."

"I don't know anything about the KGB," Kalinin told him.

"Sarkisov says otherwise," Katz replied. "Besides, I'm certain every intelligence outfit in this part of the world knows or suspects you're KGB. Of course, if you aren't KGB, none of these names will mean anything to you."

The Israeli removed a sheet of paper from his jacket pocket and handed it to Kalinin. A list of names were written in Cyrillic letters. Twenty-three of Kalinin's operatives in Mexico City.

"If you don't cooperate with us, we're going to liquidate every person on this list," Katz declared. "We're also going to give scopolamine to you and your two friends here. I'm sure you've had training to resist the drug, but we're bound to learn some new information. I understand one doesn't even remember what is said under the influence of truth serum, so you won't even know what you told us until you find yourself on trial back in Moscow."

"You'll never get away with this!" Reutov snapped. "If you kill our people, the Morkrie Dela will retaliate and liquidate CIA operatives all over the world!"

"That's not my concern," Katz lied smoothly. "I don't work for the CIA, and I don't care if the KGB assassination section kills a thousand American agents. That's not my problem and it won't be yours, either, comrade. After we get some information from you and your sleeping chum, you'll be the first KGB operatives we dispose of."

Reutov figured he had nothing to loose. He lunged at Katz, hoping to use the senior member of the group as a shield and grab his Makarov from the table. The Israeli was a head shorter and a good twenty years older than the KGB captain. Overpowering him looked easy enough.

Katz suddenly sidestepped out of Reutov's path and grabbed the Russian's nearest wrist with his left hand. His right arm slashed a short stroke and chopped the edge of his steel prosthesis under Reutov's ribs. The KGB agent groaned in pain, and Katz twisted his wrist to lock the captive arm at the elbow. Reutov bent over, and Katz kicked him in the face. The steel toe of his shoe hit the Russian on the point of the chin hard. Reutov fell unconscious to the floor.

James grabbed Kalinin from behind and jammed the muzzle of his pistol against the colonel's head to discourage him from trying anything rash. Kalinin did not try to struggle. Katz glanced down at Captain Reutov and shook his head.

"He's a bit too headstrong for this sort of work," Katz commented. He turned to Kalinin. "We really don't want to kill anyone, Colonel, but if we have to use such tactics we will."

"What's your interest in this terrorist base and the Cubans?" the KGB officer asked. "Never mind. You won't tell me, anyway."

"I'm afraid not, Colonel," the Phoenix commander confirmed. "We're really not interested in your organization here in Mexico City. If you tell us what we need to know about the terrorist base in the Yucatán, we'll let you and your comrades go. We will have to resort to scopolamine to ensure you tell us the truth and won't devise some method of clueing in the Cubans in advance."

"How do I know you won't turn over all this information to the CIA afterward?" Kalinin asked. "If you're some sort of mercenary clandestine outfit, that would be the logical follow-up. I'm sure the Americans would pay well for such information."

"This has nothing to do with money," Katz promised. "All we want are the Cubans and the terrorists. You tell us about them, and after we settle business in the Yucatán, we'll leave the country and destroy all the other information about your organization here. You have my word on that, though you don't have any reason to believe me."

"I think I'm a good judge of character," Kalinin said with a smile. "My instincts tell me you'll keep your word and question that you'd hunt down and murder twenty-three men in cold blood if I refuse. I suspect you're a warrior, but not a butcher."

"I don't have to be," Katz said grimly. "Others would handle that part of the mission if it comes to that."

"Perhaps," Kalinin said with a sigh. "You people have already succeeded in finding out who twenty-three of my people are, luring me here and putting me in a very awkward situation. I'd be an idiot to underestimate what else you're capable of. Very well, my mysterious friend. I'll tell you about Major Pescador and his base in the Yucatán jungle."

12

Maria Santo squatted by the pile of glowing ashes and blew on them gently. She prayed that she would succeed in fanning the flames. The fire had burned briefly, and she had not been able to find enough dry wood or grass to keep it alive. Everything in and near the jungle was so damn green.

The vultures had left by sundown. A small blessing, considering the new terrors that filled the night. Strange birdcalls and insect noises, chattering monkeys and chirping tree frogs, combined to create an ongoing chorus all around her. The darkness made the jungle even more sinister and fed her fearful imagination with the least rustling of leaves or sense of movement.

Every sound was filled with menace. The flapping of leathery wings overhead warned her of the swarms of bats that swooped down from the night skies to feast on the abundant supply of insects. Since hundreds of insects had been drawn to the bodies of the dead soldiers, the number of bats in the area was greater than normal.

Maria hated bats. She was afraid they would land in her hair, and she covered her head every time one of the winged creatures flew near her. She had also heard stories about bats with rabies attacking human beings and tales of the vampire bats. The flying bloodsuckers are found in South and Central America, including Mexico. She recalled conflicting stories about vampire bats. Some claimed they seldom attacked people and favored cattle and other animals to humans, but according to popular sources, the bats were capable of swarming down on a lone target and biting the neck and wrists, sucking the life from the victim until only a shallow, pale corpse remained.

Something stirred in the grass. Perhaps a rodent or a lizard, but Maria immediately thought it might be a snake. The jungle was crawling with snakes. Maria knew that several types of poisonous snakes are native to the Yucatán, and though she didn't know much about snakes, she felt an instinctive loathing and revulsion for them.

Then she heard a growling in the jungle. Maria trembled and tried to calm herself. She scanned the dark shapes of trees and bushes, and though the creature remained invisible, she heard the growl again. Maybe it was just an ocelot, Maria thought, trying to reassure herself a little bit. Her native environment was that of cities, and she knew little about wild animals.

Suddenly a terrifying and unreasonable thought came to her. What if it was not an animal? Not the conventional idea of an animal, at least. The legends of El Sisimici suddenly flooded into her head. It was supposedly a man-beast similar to the Abominable Snowman or Sasquatch. Maria had never taken such stories seriously before, but the terror in the darkness made anything seem possible.

Sisimici was known by other names in different parts of Central and South America. It had been described as a hairy, wild giant. Some of the stories about it were pretty sordid and related the killing and eating of humans, kidnapping of children and raping of women. Such tales had always seemed absurd, horror stories told around a campfire. But now Maria did not find the possibility amusing as she sat at the edge of the jungle in the dark. El Sisimici became another phantom that could be lurking in the hostile night.

Why in heaven's name was she here? Because of a stupid story those idiot newspaper publishers in Mexico City wanted? Where the hell was the army? The convoy had been attacked hours ago, yet no search party had arrived. Did they care so little for the soldiers in the military? What about the safety of a reporter? Did no one care about that? Was anyone considered important besides politicians, popes and wealthy businessmen?

She slapped a mosquito on her cheek. At least a dozen insects had bitten her. She would be lucky if she did not get malaria, yellow fever or both, but the possibility of a disease hardly mattered at that moment. Maria doubted she would live through the night anyway.

Something moved among the ferns along the road. Maria saw the vague outline of a shape among the shadows. Her eyes widened in horror when she noted the outline of a head and shoulders that appeared human. El Sisimici! Maria thought, her mind racing toward panic. She reached for a rock as the humanoid shape drew closer. Her fingers closed around the feeble weapon, and she slowly rose to her feet. Her legs trembled, and she felt she might faint. The figure advanced on two legs, back straight, arms at its sides. It appeared to carry something, but Maria could not tell what the object might be. It moved in the direction of the bodies by the trucks.

"¡No, señorita!" a voice warned from behind her. "Put down the rock before someone gets hurt."

She whirled and threw the stone in the general direction of the voice. Rafael Encizo ducked, and the rock sailed more than a foot above his head. The woman started to run, but the circulation in her legs had been cut off from sitting so long. She could barely walk, let alone run.

"Calm down!" Encizo urged, stepping closer. He held his empty palms high. "No one will hurt you. Just relax."

"Rafael!" Manuel Cassias called out cheerfully as he approached. "I see you found a woman. That figures. You always did have a knack for the ladies."

The smuggler cast the beam of a flashlight across Maria. She shielded her eyes with an arm. When Rafael stepped into the light, Maria saw the Mendoza machine gun on a shoulder strap, the holstered pistol on his hip and a combat knife sheathed on his belt. He was dressed in black camouflage uniform and boots. Maria had not even heard him approach and his cunning and weaponry frightened her, yet his voice was gentle and his expression suggested he meant her no harm.

"Get the light out of her eyes," Encizo told Cassias. "This lady looks like she's already been through the wringer."

"You know there are women terrorists," Benito Tillo remarked as he limped toward them.

"So they left her here alone and unarmed?" Encizo scoffed. "That doesn't make sense, Benito. The terrorists hit the convoy, no doubt about that, but this lady wasn't with the enemy side. A blind man could see that."

"Who is she?" Cassias inquired, then turned a questioning look in the woman's direction. *"Señorita?"*

"My name is Maria Santo and I am a newspaper reporter," she answered, slowly catching her breath after the shock of the unexpected encounter. "I was with the truck convoy. I was covering a stupid human-interest story about the military. These men attacked us. They killed everyone and they thought I was dead..."

"Here," Encizo began as he handed her his canteen. "Have some water. Relax. You're safe now. Take your time and tell us about the men who attacked the convoy. Any details you can remember about them might help us."

"Who are you?" Maria asked. "Army? *Federales?*"

"We're looking for the terrorists," Cassias answered. "Probably the same outfit that attacked these trucks."

"Twenty-third September Communist League?" Maria asked, taking a long drink of water. "I heard one of them mention it. He seemed to be the leader, but he accused the 23rd SCL group of being barbarian trash."

"He was in charge, but he wasn't a member of the terrorists?" Encizo asked eagerly.

"He acted as if he was different from the others," she recalled. "They called him *'capitán'* and he spoke Spanish with an accent . . . like yours, *señor*."

"Cuban," Encizo said with a nod. "He was in command of the *bastardos* who committed this massacre. *¡Madre de Dios!*"

Encizo turned away from the others. Tears crept down his cheeks. Poor Raul, he thought. They have made him into a murderer. My little brother is a murderer. . . .

"Rafael?" Cassias spoke softly. "They've got quite a headstart. If we're going to catch up with them, we'll have to be moving on soon."

"We can't track them in the dark anyway," Miguel, Tillo's big bearlike associate, stated in a gruff voice. "Reading signs in the jungle is difficult at all times. At night? Impossible."

"Miguel is right," Adolfo, the one-eyed gunrunner agreed. "We cannot track them until morning."

"You two are the experts," Encizo admitted. "Luis, do you know if we are close to where your friends were ambushed?"

"Yes," the young bandit answered with a nervous nod. "I know this road. My friends and I were in the jungle, about ten kilometers east of here, when we came across the terrorists."

"You think we should just head east and hope we get lucky?" Tillo asked Encizo. He snorted harshly. "I think that's a good way to get lost in the jungle,

Rafael. If we did catch up with them now, it would probably be as big a surprise for us as it would be for the terrorists. I'd like all the surprise to be for them."

"We'd have to use flashlights to track in the dark, and that would be flirting with suicide," Encizo agreed.

"If we're going to set up camp until dawn, I suggest we don't do it here," Tillo advised. "The gas tanks of these trucks have been ruptured. A match or even a spark could ignite the gasoline."

"I don't want to stay here," Maria added almost desperately.

"Don't worry," Encizo assured her, wiping his eyes. He hoped the darkness would hide his tears. "I wish we could get you out of here tonight. Unfortunately you can't leave until morning. Two of Benito's men will take you to the plane. Armando can fly you out of here. We'll decide later who will escort you."

"Wait a moment," Maria began. "You have a plane?"

"Of course," Cassias said with a small laugh. "That is how we got here. Oh, the plane is at an airstrip about twenty kilometers to the north."

"Maybe you should go with her, Manuel," Encizo suggested. "You've taken more than enough risks already. Anything you felt you owed me in the past is paid in full with interest, old friend. Now might be a good time for you to leave. You won't do us much good in the jungle, anyway. You're strictly a city person. Always have been and always will be.''

"Don't worry about me," Cassias assured him. "I can handle myself in this place. It is just like a city park only there are more trees and instead of muggers there are wild animals.''

"I'm serious, Manuel," Encizo insisted.

"You say I don't owe you anything," Cassias said with a thin smile. "I remember that night when I was strapped to a chair, helpless, waiting to be tortured and murdered. You saved me. You risked your own life for me. At the time nobody gave a damn what happened to me. I was just a small-time smuggler and nobody cared except you. When you rescued me from that nightmare, you did more than save me from a hideous and painful death, you showed me everybody in the world isn't a hustler or a savage in a great global cesspool. There was still courage and compassion great enough to put one's own life on the line for a fellow human being. I'm staying, Rafael. I have to.''

"I don't want you here," Encizo said in a firm voice.

"I'm not doing this for you," Cassias switched to English, hoping the others would not understand him. "Fuck what you want, man. I'm doing this for *me*.''

"You're full of shit," Encizo replied in English. He switched back to Spanish and added, "Let's find some place to set up camp for the night."

13

Fong was an expert in the use of the machete. He carried two big jungle knives, one sheathed at each hip. The Chinese-Mexican gunrunner also carried a pair of 9 mm Largo pistols in a double-shoulder rig with a gun holstered under each arm. He used the machetes like a thrashing machine. Fong moved with each cut, his body gracefully adding power to every slash. The circular strokes and concentration of movement had been learned by years of training in *chuan fa* martial arts.

He chopped down ferns, vines and other plants to make a larger clearing for their campsite. Rafael Encizo and his odd collection of allies built a big lean-to with ponchos and tree limbs. When they finished, the shelter was sort of an open-end tent. Maria could not recall seeing anything more inviting after spending several hours alone in the jungle.

"I'd say we've all worked up an appetite," Encizo announced. He sat down and opened his backpack. "Are you hungry, Maria?"

"Yes," she replied, a bit surprised to discover she felt like she could eat despite the horrors she had witnessed and experienced. "I would like some food."

"We've got some beef jerky, and we'll cook some frijoles, a few corn meal tortillas and a pot of coffee," Manuel Cassias declared with a grin. "How's that sound?"

"Excellent!" she said with a nod. "Are you sure it is safe to build a fire? The terrorists..."

"They wouldn't be very close or they would have already seen the glow of the little fire you made," Benito Tillo announced as he started to pour water into a blue metal coffeepot. "We saw it about a kilometer away. Besides, the terrorists would not stay in the immediate area where they had attacked the convoy. Those trucks and the soldiers are meant to be a calling card. A grisly announcement of the beginning of a new wave of terrorism by the 23rd SCL. There was no other reason to attack the convoy. They did not take anything from the trucks. The slaughter simply served as a message."

"It is terrible," Maria said, and shook her head in dismay. "Now you men are hunting the terrorists. How did you know about them? Who are you working for?"

"Maria," Encizo began with a sigh. "I know you are a newspaper reporter, but we don't want this in print. We could all get in a lot of trouble with the authorities if this became public knowledge. We're breaking a number of laws with this little venture. We don't have badges, warrants, permits to carry guns or any legal right to be doing this. We could all go to prison if we get caught.''

''Why didn't you tell the *federales*?'' she asked. ''Let the army deal with the terrorists. It is their job.''

''We have reasons,'' Encizo assured her. ''I have a very personal reason, which I can't explain. All I can say is that it's something I have to handle myself. It is a family matter.''

''I don't really understand,'' Maria confessed. ''But I owe you gentlemen my life. I will not betray you by printing such information in the newspaper, Rafael.''

''Don't call me Rafael in the article,'' Encizo urged with a smile. ''Make it Juan, Roberto or Norman. Don't use any of our real names and keep the descriptions vague. Fair enough?''

''I can't see much in the dark, anyway.'' She smiled as the flames of the campfire illuminated Encizo's face. ''You could tell me not to write about it at all.''

''It's a good story, and you'll write about it,'' Encizo stated. ''That's your job. Right now, this is our job. We can't explain it and perhaps it might not make much sense even if we could, but it's something we have to do.''

"Perhaps I'd have an even better story if I went with you after the terrorists," Maria remarked.

"Haven't you had enough adventure?" Cassias asked with a chuckle. "Besides, you're too pretty. We'd spend all our time looking at you, and we wouldn't even see the terrorists until it was too late. It's too dangerous to take you with us. Have some mercy on us, eh?"

"That's difficult to argue with," Maria laughed. She was surprised by the sound of her own voice. "An hour ago I would have sworn I would never laugh again."

"I know the feeling," Encizo assured her. "You have survived a difficult ordeal, Maria. It required courage and self-control. You met the challenge and survived. Take pride in it. You're a stronger person now. Take that strength with you when you leave here."

She stared at Encizo's eyes. They were warm and gentle, yet she saw some trace of wild passion in those eyes and wisdom born of harsh experience. Maria was very drawn to him. If things were different...

"I'll be going with you to the airstrip in the morning," Tillo said with a sigh. "I think I'll take Adolfo with us. That will leave you with Miguel and Fong. They're very good men, and they can handle themselves in a fight."

"It's your decision, Benito," Encizo said. "We would welcome your courage and ability if you choose to stay, but someone really does have to see to Maria's safety."

"No need to help me protect my honor," Tillo assured him. "Fact is, I think it is time for me to go home and retire from this crazy stuff and just run my businesses. My hip hurts, my whole body is sore, and I'm just not up to this. My bullfighting days were over years ago and they are *still* over. I know that now and I'm not about to risk anyone's life—yours or mine—to try to prove something that just isn't true anymore."

"Being able to accept that probably takes more courage than going on into the jungle, my friend," Cassias said as he placed a hand on Tillo's shoulder.

"Quit talking and fix the food," Tillo said with mock gruffness. "I'm hungry enough to eat these trees if you don't hurry up."

"*Si, si,*" Cassias replied. "We can't have you chewing down the trees."

After the meal they rested. The men took turns standing watch while the others slept. Maria lay next to Encizo, their backs touching. She drifted off to sleep occasionally, but awoke at intervals to the shriek of a night bird or the growling of an animal. She was also thinking of the man next to her. Rafael was handsome, courageous, understanding and mysterious. An irresistible combination for a young woman like Maria. What were his secrets? What was the man really like? Some stirring of her senses told her that he could be an exciting lover.

Miguel completed a two-hour watch and woke Encizo to take the final shift, from 3:00 a.m. till daybreak. The big Mexican gunrunner curled up under the lean-to and went to sleep almost the instant his head touched the ground. Encizo stretched his muscles, gathered up his Mendoza subgun and stood. The jungle was an immense and unfathomable darkness, and his eyes adjusted slowly, but vision was minimal. It seemed, though, that there was no immediate danger. The night animals sounded a bit strange, but other nights in other jungles made Encizo understand there was no real menace in the noises. Most animals try to avoid man. In fact he would have been far more concerned if the noise stopped. It would signal the approach of something that frightened the animals.

"Rafael," Maria called softly as she sat up. "May I speak with you a moment?"

"You ought to get as much sleep as you can," he told her. "And I have to stay alert while on guard duty or I'll get fired."

"You seem to be in charge," she stated.

"Then I'd have to fire myself," he said with a grin. "What's on your mind, Maria?"

"I'm being taken out of here in the morning and you're going after the terrorists," Maria explained.

"There's a chance we won't see each other after that. While the others are asleep, I wanted to personally thank you for everything and wish you good luck tomorrow."

"Gracias," he said, gently touching her cheek, "but the others were as responsible for taking you in as I am. I wish you good luck, too. A lady in the city needs it."

"I'm engaged to be married in three months," Maria said as she took a small business card from a pocket and handed it to Encizo. "I'm not sure if I'll go through with it now. I'm not sure what I'll do after this is over."

"You still have the rest of your life to make those decisions," the Cuban told her.

"I know," she said, "but take my card and contact me someday. I don't know what I'll be doing or who I'll be with, but I want to see you again."

"No promises," Encizo replied, putting the card in a pocket, "but I'll try if I can."

She leaned closer and offered her lips. He kissed her, and as her lips parted, the contact became more lingering and exploratory. There was a hint of passion in her kiss, and Encizo wanted to savor it. He would have liked to take the woman somewhere private and allow their mutual desire to run its natural course.

But it was the wrong time, Encizo realized, and the wrong place. Maybe there would be another time, another place, and things would be different. Actually he had learned long ago that trying to predict the future was folly. People and circumstances often change a lot with the passing of time. When Maria left the Yucatán, she would go on with her life. There was little chance Encizo would see her again.

Their lips parted. Encizo stepped back and Maria lay back on the ground under the lean-to. A few minutes later she was asleep, and Rafael Encizo stood guard until dawn. His thoughts kept him company, thoughts about Maria and other women he had known in the past. He recalled missions with Phoenix Force and his close friendship with the other four members of the elite commando team. He wondered if a mission had come up and Brognola had tried to contact him. They were probably puzzled about where he had gone and why.

Most of all, he thought about his brother. Captain Raul Encizo would probably regard him as an enemy and might try to kill him on sight. Somehow Raul had to be protected and had to learn they were brothers who had been separated since childhood. It was most important that it be explained to Raul that he was serving the same people who had murdered their parents.

Of course, he might not get a chance. Rafael Encizo could meet his end in a number of ways before getting an opportunity to present his case to Raul. And not many would know or really care if Rafael

Encizo died, he thought calmly. Brognola and Phoenix Force would care. The others connected with Stony Man wouldn't be indifferent, but Encizo had never been as close to them as the other members of his own team. Phoenix Force would find a replacement, the way Calvin James had joined the team when Keio Ohara had been killed. Probably with Karl Hahn or John Trent. Both were good men, highly skilled professionals who had worked with Phoenix Force in the past.

He had come to Mexico to find his brother, and he was getting closer to that goal. Part of him wanted to turn back, he admitted to himself, because the more he learned about Captain Encizo, the more painful the truth became. Raul was a dedicated killing machine for the Communists, Rafael Encizo's oldest and most despised enemies. Yet there was still a glimmer of hope from what Maria had told him. Raul still had a sense of decency. He realized the 23rd SCL terrorists were unprincipled scum, and he had warned them that he would not tolerate any of his men committing rape or torture.

It was a faint hope, but it was all Rafael had to try to convince himself that his mission was not as hopeless as it seemed.

AT DAYBREAK they brewed a fresh pot of coffee. Everyone had a cup as they struck camp and loaded up their backpacks. Benito Tillo, Maria Santo, and Armando prepared to head north to the plane.

"We'll drop Maria off at a small airport I know which keeps discreet records concerning landing aircraft," Tillo explained. "I'll get a car there and drive her to a nearby city where she can get in touch with whatever authorities she wants to and get picked up. Armando and Adolfo are to refuel the plane and come back for you. They will be at the prearranged airstrip when you're ready to leave."

"That sounds fine," Encizo replied. "I appreciate everything you've done, Benito. There's no way I can properly thank you. We never could have done this without your help."

"You take care of the terrorists," Tillo replied. "I don't want them messing up my country. When this is over, you come to Tijuana, and we'll go have a good time with lots of drinking and wild women. That's the kind of adventure I plan to have in the future."

"*¡Vaya con Dios!*" Cassias stated, shaking hands with Tillo. "If I don't see you again, good luck and keep out of trouble."

Tillo suddenly embraced Cassias. "Don't get killed," he said softly. "Even if you never agreed to smuggle guns for me, you're still a friend of mine."

"I'll do my best to stay alive," Cassias assured him. "How can I get drunk and chase whores with you if I'm dead, eh?"

"We'd better go," Tillo announced. Adolfo nodded in agreement. "Maria, you ready?"

"Si," the woman confirmed. She fixed her eyes on Rafael Encizo. "I don't think there's anything I can say except I'll never forget any of you or what you did for me. Good luck and let me know what happens."

"We will," Encizo promised. *"Adiós."*

"Adiós," she replied with a weak smile, and with that, they headed up the road.

The others watched until they were out of sight. Then Cassias, who stood next to Encizo, poured the contents of his cup into the Cuban's. Encizo tapped his cup against his friend's in a silent gesture of thanks.

"That's the last of the pot," Cassias declared. "I think we've got enough left for one more brew. I hope we find the enemy base before we run out because I'm just no damn good without my morning coffee."

"Well, we won't find them standing around here," Encizo commented. He drank from the cup and grimaced. Half the contents were coffee grounds. "Let's get going."

14

"¡Buenos días!" Guillermo Arrozco announced cheerfully as the strangers began to climb from the station wagon parked in front of his office. Of the five, at least three appeared to be either *norteamericanos* or *europeos*. One of the men was black and Arrozco guessed he was probably from *los Estados Unidos*. "Good morning. I speak English, if that will be good for you."

"Makes my bloody day, mate," David McCarter muttered sourly. The Briton had spent the last five hours behind the steering wheel of the wagon, and it had not improved his disposition.

"We heard about your air service," Yakov Katzenelenbogen began, gazing at the small airfield. A single helicopter sat on a bald patch of earth. "It sounded ideal for our purposes."

"I hope so, I hope so," Arrozco said with a smile, nodding as he spoke. "It is a hundred pesos for each passenger for a regular tour flight. More than that if you want to go somewhere in particular."

"We're planning to go into the jungle," Gary Manning stated. The brawny Canadian had two large duffel bags slung over his shoulder. Both were full and jointly weighed at least two hundred and fifty pounds, but the burden did not seem to bother Manning.

"All of you?" Arrozco said. "Are you sure you all want to go? It would be very expensive."

"I'd like to go back to Mexico City," Ricardo Vasquez commented under his breath. The four strangers had proved to be more than he had bargained for. Vasquez was afraid they would get him killed before he could collect the rest of the fee they had promised him.

"¿Que?" Arrozco inquired.

"No importa, señor," Vasquez assured him.

"Nice chopper," Calvin James commented. "You could carry ten or twelve people in that baby."

"Si," Arrozco confirmed. "In fact the helicopter has a capacity for fourteen passengers. It is a Brazilian type called *El Aguila*, designed as a military transport aircraft. I understand it is modeled after a helicopter in the United States."

"The Bell UH-1," David McCarter stated with a nod. "Does this Aguila handle the same as the Bell? Same controls? Same flight range and general level of fuel consumption?"

"I have never flown a Bell," Arrozco said with a shrug, "but I would imagine the Aguila is very similar. Are you a pilot, *señor*?"

"I've flown a few choppers," the Briton remarked.

"And crashed a couple," Manning muttered, recalling occasions when an aircraft had suffered because McCarter had to land in a hurry.

"I'm never going to hear the end of that," McCarter growled. He turned his attention back to Arrozco. "What kind of shape is she in? Looks all ready to go."

"Perfect shape and all fueled," Arrozco answered. "Of course, we must charter each flight and get permission from the federal air traffic and communications. Still, I can probably book your flight for some time tomorrow."

"I'm sorry, but we'll need it today," Katz said with a shrug. "We'll pay you a hundred thousand pesos."

"That is most generous, *señor*," Arrozco said, his eyes wide with surprise. "But I will have to wait for my partner to return with the other helicopter and arrange with my secretary and repair crew...."

"Give the man his money," Katz instructed.

"Here you go, *amigo*," James said as he handed Arrozco a valise. "A hundred thousand pesos. Count it for yourself."

"This is very . . . very much money," Arrozco said awkwardly. "Still I can't . . ."

"I'm afraid you'll have to," Katz told him, drawing his Beretta from his jacket. "We're borrowing your chopper. I'm really very sorry about this, but you are making a nice profit. If the aircraft becomes damaged or wrecked, we'll send you payment for it."

"Unless we all get killed," James said with a sigh. "There's a fifty-fifty chance that might happen. We might have to leave it in the jungle, anyway. If we came back here you might have the *federales* waiting for us. Life can be a real bitch sometimes, but we'll try not to mess up your chopper."

"Is that including bullet holes?" Manning wondered aloud. "Let's go find the secretary and maintenance people. We'll have to lock you folks up for a while and put all your communications out of action. Telephone, shortwave, whatever."

"Sorry, mate," McCarter told Arrozco. The Briton drew his Browning as he spoke. "I know this is a pain in the arse, but nobody will get hurt if you don't give us any difficulty. When your partner comes back, he'll let you blokes out, and you can do whatever you want with a hundred thousand pesos that you don't need to tell the tax collectors about."

"I—I am confused," Arrozco confessed. "You are stealing my helicopter, no?"

"Don't get technical, buddy," James told him. "We got enough trouble already without having to explain this to you. We're borrowing it against your will, but it ain't really stealing because we're good guys. *¿Comprende?*"

"*No comprendo,*" Arrozco said, shaking his head.

"I'm not sure we understand it, either," Katz said with a sigh. "But we're doing it anyway."

THE YUCATÁN JUNGLE did not look like much on the map, but it seemed endless for Rafael Encizo and his four remaining allies. Not that the Yucatan was a "green hell" as one might describe the Amazon or the Congo. The tropical rain forest consisted of tall grass, ferns, a variety of plants and thousands of trees, many of them valuable hardwoods. Dozens of colorful and exotic birds lived among the branches. Canaries and finches sang excited warnings as the men approached. The suspicious parrots remained perched on tree limbs and watched the intruders. One young yellow-head Amazon spread its wings and opened its hook-bill beak in a hissing threat. Older, wiser parrots knew better than to draw attention to themselves. The birds realized the best choice of action was simply to wait for a potential threat to pass.

"This is the area, *señor*," Luis announced as they approached a shallow creek surrounded by palms and nut trees. "This is where the terrorists attacked us."

"Are you sure, Luis?" Manuel Cassias asked. "It happened some time ago, and this area looks much the same as other parts of the jungle."

"I am certain," the young bandit insisted. "My *amigos* and I saw them over there among the ebony trees."

He pointed to a cluster of trees on the other side of the creek. Encizo moved to some of the larger palm trees near the bank where they stood. He noticed one trunk had been scarred by something that chipped bark and gouged wood.

"You used these trees for cover?" the Cuban asked, indicating the palms.

"*Si,*" Luis confirmed. "I remember the sound of bullets hitting the trees as we crouched behind them."

"This seems to be the right place," Encizo said with a nod. "I wonder how much farther we'll have to go to find their base."

"Rafael, Manuel," Miguel said as he knelt by the edge of the bank. The big man brushed back some tall grass with the back of his hand. "I think you should see this."

Encizo and Cassias joined Miguel and gazed down at his discovery. The tracker had found several bootprints in the moist earth along the creek.

"Do you think the terrorists made those tracks?" Encizo asked.

"I'm sure of it," Miguel replied with a confident nod. "I examined the bootprints by the road for hours to memorize the shapes and sizes, the marks left by the pattern of the soles of the boots and blank spots caused by the wear and tear of the soles after years of use. I recognize some of these prints. Most are pretty confused, and one on top of the other. Still, a few prints are clear, and I have no doubt about them.''

"All the toes are pointed at the creek," Encizo noticed. "So they must have crossed it or maybe waded either downstream or upstream to try to avoid leaving a sign for anybody to track them."

"That's what I figure, too," Miguel told him. "The grass here has been trampled flat. Grass springs back up after somebody steps on it. That might take a few minutes or hours or even days. Depends on how many people stepped on it, how long it is, how wet it is. Ground is damp and the grass is wet from moisture retained in the area because of the umbrella formed by tree branches. Hard to say how long the prints have been here."

"Any idea how many of them we're trying to find?" Cassias inquired, not sure he wanted to know the answer.

"At least a dozen," Miguel said with a shrug. "Maybe closer to two dozen. I haven't been able to read much sign on them so far. I'd have to go over the ground for more than an hour to give you greater detail."

"Time is something we might not have much of," Encizo told him. "These *hombres* must suspect that somebody will go into the jungle after them. That means they'll probably abandon the base they're at now and set up elsewhere as soon as possible."

"We might cross the creek and check for tracks on the other side," Fong commented. He had just joined the others and heard part of the conversation. He was a man of few words, and the others were almost startled to hear him talk. "Perhaps we'll be lucky."

"Sounds like a logical place to start," Encizo agreed. "What do you say, Miguel?"

"Si," the big man stated as he started to rise. "Still, don't get your hopes too high. The terrorists are probably fifty or sixty kilometers from here by now—"

Miguel's words were abruptly cut off, and his head snapped back as the crack of a rifle shot echoed within the forest. A scarlet bullet hole appeared in his forehead, and the exit wound opened up the back of his skull, spewing blood and brains onto the ground. Encizo immediately dove to the ground and rolled toward the palm trees. He heard more rifle shots and the deranged metal-woodpecker sound of full-auto weapons. Bullets splattered mud from the soggy earth.

There was a scream. Encizo did not know who had been hit, but the voice was nearby. It had to belong to one of his companions. The Cuban lay on his side to slip the Mendoza's strap from his shoulder. He could see little except the tall grass by the bank and the vague shapes of the ebony trees. The enemy was somewhere among those trees on the opposite side of the creek.

He placed the Mendoza in the crooks of his elbows and low-crawled to the shelter of a large palm tree. A bullet struck the tree trunk as Enzizo slithered to its base. Luis was sprawled behind another tree. The front of the young bandit's shirt was stained with blood. He was pale and trembling with fear and held a hand to his bullet-torn chest. Blood seeped between his fingers.

"Luis!" Enzizo shouted to be heard above the roar of gunfire. "Luis, can you hear me?"

"Si," the youth replied weakly. His face contorted with pain, and blood drooled from his lips.

"Don't try to talk," Enzizo urged, aware that Luis was badly hurt. Probably shot through a lung, he thought. "Just stay where you are. Don't move around, or you might bleed to death. Understand?"

Luis nodded in reply.

Enzizo peered around the tree trunk. Several figures in jungle camouflage fatigues approached from the trees. Others fired from cover among the trees. Standard tactic, Enzizo realized. Try to pin down the opponents with gunfire while covering the advance of troops.

"Rafael!" a familiar voice called from the bank of the creek. "Are you all right?"

Encizo turned to see Manuel Cassias sprawled beside Miguel's body. The dead man had been the closest cover available when the shooting started. Several bullets had smashed into the dead body, and at least one had struck Cassias just above the left knee. He lay on his right side, his shattered leg extended in an awkward position. Cassias braced his pump-action shotgun across the corpse and pointed it at the enemy.

"Hold your fire!" Encizo told him. "They're not within range!"

"They're close enough—damn near put a bullet up my ass!" Cassias shouted back. "What the hell should we do now?"

"Hold on," Encizo answered. He glanced about for Fong, but didn't spot him. "You have any grenades?"

"A couple," Cassias confirmed. "I don't like these things, Rafael. I never used one before..."

"Just pull the pin and throw it," Encizo replied. He flinched as a chunk of bark was chipped from the tree trunk by another stray bullet. "Throw the grenade, *not* the pin. Okay?"

"Nobody likes a smartass," Cassias muttered, and took a grenade from his belt.

"Don't throw it yet," Encizo instructed. He turned back to Luis and asked, "Do you have a grenade?"

The wounded youth nodded weakly and held up an arm. An M-26 hand grenade was in his fist. Encizo nodded his approval. He glanced at the advancing enemy troops. The uniformed figures moved forward slowly, trying to make the most of trees and bushes for cover. The Cuban Phoenix Force pro counted five men, but there may have been more. The cover fire was clearly the action of more than one undetected opponent.

"All right," Encizo began. "When I lob the first grenade at the enemy, you two throw your grenades, as well. If the explosions drive them down to the creek, be ready with that shotgun, Manuel."

"Just do it," Cassias urged.

The Cuban yanked the pin from a grenade and hurled it across the creek at the enemy. The green-gray metal ball landed among some ferns near a clump of undergrowth the terrorists used for cover. Cassias threw another M-26 a half second later, eager to get rid of the dreaded and unfamiliar explosive. It fell on the enemy side of the creek, roughly eighty meters from where Encizo's grenade landed.

Luis rolled away from the palm tree and hurled a grenade with what little strength he could muster. It splashed into the middle of the creek, but he did not notice. He had begun to vomit blood and pink foam from lung tissue. The young man thrashed about on the ground from the violent heavings. A burst of Kalashnikov bullets tore into him before he could reach cover and high-velocity projectiles raked his shoulders and upper back. The auxiliary artery was severed, the brachial plexus ruptured and his spinal cord snapped. Luis convulsed for a moment, then sprawled motionless on the ground in the final serenity of death.

The grenades exploded. Some of the terrorists who had seen the sinister metal balls and guessed what they were bolted for safety. But two terrorists were too close when Encizo's grenade blew, and the fragmentation explosion killed one man instantly and hurled what was left of his body nine feet. The blast ripped off the right arm of the other terrorist. He fell to the ground. Torrents of blood gushed from the ragged remains of his ravaged shoulder.

One terrorist reached for the grenade Cassias had thrown. His fingertips touched the M-26 the instant it exploded. The blast literally tore his head off. The decapitated corpse fell near another pair who were not accustomed to dealing with opponents who could fight back. They ran forward and dove for safety in the waters of the creek.

Luis's grenade exploded at that moment. The terrorists were blown to bits as they hit the water, and ravaged parts were scattered across the creek. Grisly chunks landed along the shore. The sight unnerved some of the enemy, who started to retreat for more solid cover.

Encizo aimed his Mendoza and opened fire. A salvo of 9 mm parabellum rounds slammed into the backs of two retreating terrorists. The pair collapsed, their spines wrecked and internal organs punctured. Another terrorist turned and swung his AK-47 toward Encizo's position. The Phoenix Force pro nailed him with a trio of 115-grain projectiles in the chest. The man tumbled backward as he triggered his Kalashnikov and fired a few bullets into the sky in a final dying gesture.

The remaining terrorists ducked behind cover and fired back at Encizo and Cassias. The Cuban warrior dove from behind the palm tree, hit the ground in a shoulder roll and tumbled to the tree trunk formerly used by Luis for protection. Most of the terrorists were still concentrating on Encizo's original position when he poked the barrel of the Mendoza around the trunk and fired another volley.

Bullets raked a leafy green bush. A man suddenly jumped up from behind it with both hands clutched to his throat. A 9 mm round had caught him in the neck and torn open the carotid before it struck vertebrae. The terrorist's eyes rolled up into his head, and his body crumpled to the earth.

Cassias fumbled with another hand grenade. He barely noticed the pain in his bullet-shattered leg. The excitement and terror of the confrontation consumed his every thought and emotion, though he was feverish from the wound and his hands were unsteady as he pulled the pin.

"*¡Mierda!*" a terrorist exclaimed when he saw Cassias about to throw the grenade and swung the muzzle of his weapon around.

Cassias hurled the grenade as the terrorist opened fire with his Kalashnikov. Three slugs plowed into the upper torso of Manuel Cassias. The smuggler flopped back on the ground, and his body twitched violently on the muddy surface. His grenade landed behind the gunman who had shot him. The terrorist turned and desperately searched the ground for the M-26. He used the barrel of his AK-47 to brush aside some ferns and stared down at the grenade. His eyes widened in terror as he realized he was about to die.

The grenade exploded inches from his feet. The blast of fragmentation shrapnel disemboweled the terrorist and shattered his sternum and ribcage. Bone splinters were driven inward to pierce his heart and lungs. The man's ragged, bloodied corpse was thrown ten feet by the blast and fell to the earth near Pedro Garcia. The big terrorist recoiled from the gory corpse and tripped over a tree root. He grunted as he fell gracelessly on his backside.

"Garcia!" Captain Raul Encizo called out. "Are you hit?"

"No," the 23rd SCL thug replied gruffly, "but one of my comrades looks like a sieve from a grenade blast. We've lost a lot of men, *Capitán*. There are only five opponents, but the way they fight, they must be devils."

"They are not devils, Garcia," the Cuban officer informed him. "They are simply better armed and able to fight back, unlike the other opponents you've fought in the past. That was the reason for your training, little comrade. Did you think it would always be as easy as that butchery at the truck convoy?"

"The mighty warrior from Havana speaks," Garcia snorted. "If you are such a wonderful professional, we should have already wiped them out by now."

"If I had real soldiers, we would have," Raul Encizo said dryly. "Don't panic, Garcia. We already killed three of them. Perhaps four. That means we only need to take out one or two opponents. We still have ten men. Five to one odds should be enough of an edge even for your people."

"You're with us, too, *Capitán*," Garcia reminded him. "So far you've stayed out of the fighting and simply given orders and let the rest of us take all the risks."

"I'm in command," the captain replied. "A leader can't afford the luxury of personal heroism. However, I have an idea that will require some risk on my part. Selfish thing for me to do because if I get killed the rest of the troops will be under your command,

and they certainly won't have a prayer of survival then."

"How clever," Garcia sneered. "What's your plan, Comrade Captain?"

"You and three other comrades will fire at the trees where the man with the submachine gun is located," Raul Encizo instructed. "Keep him pinned down while I lead the rest of our forces in a charge across the creek. When we get to the other side, we'll be able to trap the enemy in a cross fire and chop him to pieces."

"That sounds good to me," Garcia admitted. "But these aren't a harmless little band of archaeologists or even a group of bandits. They fight like soldiers even if they do not wear uniforms. They may have reinforcements on the way."

"I have already radioed our home base for backup troops," the captain stated. "Major Pescador has assured me that he'll send twenty-five or thirty troops to reinforce us in case the enemy receives help. In the meantime, we only have one or two opponents left to deal with. This encounter is already an embarrassment, and I don't care to have to face Pescador and explain why we failed to take out the last members of this tiny band of opponents."

"I doubt if Pescador would do any better if he was here with fifty men," Garcia muttered. "Your major is a desk commander and never should have been sent here in the first place."

"It isn't our place to question the decisions of the state," Raul Encizo told him, but for once he agreed with Garcia. "Let's get ready."

15

A swarm of high-velocity bullets slammed into the palm trees and tore up earth near Rafael Encizo's position. The Cuban crouched low behind the trunk of the tree he used for cover. Bark chips and splinters showered down on his head and shoulders as he shoved a fresh magazine into his Mendoza.

"Sons of bitches are trying to pin me down," he muttered through clenched teeth, well aware of what the enemy strategy had to be.

The shooting was too wild, too random to be a concentrated effort to take him out. Bullets were spraying trees and bushes twenty feet from Encizo's position. The terrorists obviously did not know his exact location. That meant they were trying to keep him busy while other members of the enemy unit moved into a better position to take him out.

"Manuel!" Encizo rasped when he saw Cassias's body sprawled by the creek bank. The Mexican-American's chest was riddled by bullets. "Oh, God, Manuel."

An explosion erupted about thirty feet to Encizo's left. Clumps of dirt and pieces of wood pelted him. He ducked his head, shielding his face with the frame of his subgun, and braced himself against the tree. One of the terrorists had lobbed a grenade, and more were sure to follow. A second explosion, near the first, confirmed his expectations.

Encizo saw a metal egg with a steel stem hit the ground near his right knee. A Soviet F-1 hand grenade, he noticed as he quickly scooped it up and tossed the grenade into the creek. It exploded harmlessly, throwing gallons of water and lumps of mud into the sky. The shooting continued. Encizo held his fire, convinced the real threat would come from another direction.

He wished the other members of Phoenix Force had been with him. Cassias and the pitiful collection of gunrunners and poor Luis had not been trained or experienced enough to take on the sort of odds they had encountered in the Yucatán. Guilt tugged at Encizo's mind. He never should have let Cassias get involved in this mess. He should have protected all of them from a combat situation that only he could have predicted—and he had failed....

Encizo forced the notions into the back of his mind. There was no time for such thoughts. Survival would require all his concentration. His eyes narrowed when he saw six shapes emerge from the clump of ebony trees and dash across the creek. The uniformed figures carried AK-47s. The real attack force was closing in. He pointed the Mendoza at the enemy.

"Raul," Encizo whispered as he recognized the man leading the group. His finger froze on the trigger, afraid to open fire for fear of hitting his own brother.

Suddenly another figure bolted from the bank at the rear of Raul's terrorist hit team. It was Fong, who had waited for the enemy to close in before making his move. The gunrunner had concealed himself, even from Rafael Encizo and the others, until that moment. He rose up behind the last man in the terrorist group, a machete in each fist.

Fong swung the first blow at the back of his nearest opponent's neck. The heavy blade cleaved through muscle and bone. The 23rd SCL flunky was dead before he knew what happened, his spinal cord severed at the brain stem. Another terrorist turned as his slain comrade fell. Fong slapped the blade of one machete across the man's rifle to deflect the aim of the barrel and plunged the other jungle knife deep into his chest.

Bellowing in agony, the wounded man triggered his Kalashnikov. The burst fired six slugs into the water, three of which drilled through the leg of another terrorist. The man shrieked, dropped his AK-47 and clutched his bullet-shattered leg. Fong released the handle of the machete stuck in the chest of his second opponent and allowed the dead man to splash into the creek. His other blade slashed a deft stroke under the chin of the wounded terrorist. The sharp edge sliced open the man's throat with a single stroke.

Rafael Encizo saw Raul and the two remaining terrorists swing their weapons toward Fong. He could not use the Mendoza without risk to the lives of both Raul and Fong. Encizo swiftly drew his P-85 from shoulder leather, snapped off the safety and aimed the pistol at the two men accompanying his brother.

Fong had yanked one of his Largo pistols from its holster and hurled the machete at his opponents. Raul ducked, and the jungle knife whistled overhead like a big steel boomerang. The tactic was meant to distract and disorient the enemy rather than claim a target. Fong's fighting style was bold and unorthodox, but not very practical. A terrorist triggered his Kalashnikov and shot Fong point-blank in the stomach.

Encizo fired his Ruger. A 9 mm round slammed into the skull of the man who had shot the Chinese-Mexican. Fong had fallen backward into the water, but managed to draw his other Largo autoloader. The terrorist with the head wound splashed into the water next to Fong as Raul blasted a salvo of Kalashnikov rounds into Fong's bleeding body. The gunrunner's final act was to fire both Largo pistols.

One gun was clogged with water and burst apart in his fist. The other fired a bullet at Raul Encizo. The slug whined against the frame of the Cuban officer's assault rifle. Raul gasped with surprise and, thrown off balance, fell against the bank.

Rafael Encizo triggered the P-85 twice more and drilled both parabellums into the chest of the last man in his brother's kill squad. The man collapsed in the water to join the other corpses. Crimson streaked the creek as the bodies bobbed along the surface.

"Drop the gun, Raul!" Encizo ordered, the Ruger aimed at the captain. "The barrel is clogged with mud anyway."

Raul Encizo glanced at the barrel of his AK-47 and saw that this was true. He had jammed the muzzle into the muddy bank when he'd stumbled. He threw down his rifle and stared at Rafael Encizo, not raising his arms in surrender as he stepped onto the bank. His eyes widened when he recognized Rafael as the man whom he had encountered in Colombia. The strange man who knew his name and who had refused to kill him when they'd first met in the South American jungle two years before.

"You," Raul hissed, his hand resting on the button-flap holster on his hip. "Who are you?"

"I am Rafael Encizo," the other man replied, lowering his pistol. "Your older brother."

Raul stared at him with disbelief. Rafael returned his P-85 to the shoulder holster under his arm. The Mendoza hung from the strap, its muzzle pointed at the ground. Raul clawed open the holster on his hip and gripped the Makarov side arm. His brother did not attempt to stop him.

"You're a liar!" Raul spat, drawing his pistol. "I have no brother...."

"You must remember, Raul," Rafael insisted. "You were only five years old when we were separated. Try to remember. Our mother and father? Our sisters and your two older brothers. Juan was killed when the soldiers came and Rafael escaped. *I* escaped...."

"Lying traitor!" Raul pointed his Makarov at Rafael's face. "This is a CIA trick!"

"I won't fight you, Raul," Encizo declared, and dropped the Mendoza on the ground to prove it. "I cannot kill my only family. Can you?"

"I have no family," Raul stated. He still had his pistol aimed at Rafael. "I'm an orphan. The state is my family."

"You think Castro had you hatched from an egg, Raul?" Encizo demanded. "I have to tell you what happened to our parents and our siblings. You have to listen...."

"*¡Capitán!*" Pedro Garcia called out as he waded across the creek with his rifle pointed at Rafael Encizo. "This is the last one, eh? We are taking him prisoner or what?"

Three other terrorists accompanied Garcia. One man stepped forward and jammed the barrel of his Kalashnikov into the small of Rafael's back. The Cuban Phoenix Force commando looked at Raul's hard gaze and slowly raised his hands. He did not resist as the terrorist took his Ruger, combat knife and grenades.

"We can cut him up a little and make him talk," Garcia remarked. "Sounded like he said he was your brother. I'd like to hear more about that."

Raul glared at Garcia. He holstered his Makarov and slowly approached Rafael. The captain's eyes burned with hatred as he peered at his brother's face. Raul suddenly lashed out with his booted foot and kicked Rafael Encizo between the legs. The Phoenix fighter gasped in agony and doubled up. He dropped to one knee and started to lower his arms, but the gun muzzle at his spine convinced him to keep his hands in plain view.

"He's a liar," Raul stated, and spat on his brother's bowed head.

"Si," Garcia snickered. "I hate liars."

He slammed a boot into Rafael's ribs. The kick sent Encizo sprawling on his side. Another terrorist kicked him in the stomach. Rafael moaned, coughed violently and threw up on the grass. Garcia chuckled and prepared to launch another kick.

"¡Basta!" Raul snapped. "That's enough. We can't interrogate him if you kill him. Major Pescador will want to supervise the interrogation personally. Bring him. We'll take this *bastardo* to the base and decide what to do with him then."

"We'll handle your 'brother' with care, *Capitán*." Garcia laughed as he reached down and grabbed Rafael Encizo's shirt and hauled him to his feet. "Can you walk, or do we drag you twenty kilometers?"

"I'll...walk," Encizo croaked hoarsely. "The hell with it. Let's get it over with."

Garcia backhanded him across the mouth. Rafael's head bounced from the blow, and a ribbon of blood appeared from his lower lip, but he barely felt the pain. He was numb from the beating and the emotional trauma of seeing his friends die and finally confronting his brother to find the effort was in vain. At that moment he did not give a damn if they killed him or not.

"It won't be over for you right away, *chico*," Garcia hissed. "Before we're finished, you'll beg us to kill you."

"Whatever you say," Encizo replied wearily. "Can we go now?"

"Tie his hands behind his back and keep an eye on him," Raul ordered. "Don't underestimate this one. Hurry up. We've wasted enough time here."

16

"I found it!" Gary Manning announced in a loud voice so he would be heard above the whirling roar of the rotor blade. The Canadian lowered his binoculars and pointed at the treetops below.

The helicopter hovered above the jungle, with David McCarter expertly piloting the craft. Manning was in the seat beside him, while Katz, James and Vasquez rode in the carriage of the chopper. All five men were in jungle camouflage fatigues, paratrooper boots and an assortment of head gear. Weapons and other equipment were strapped to their bodies or within easy reach.

"Careful, David!" Katz called out. "Not too close! We want them to think we're just passing by!"

"And I thought we might drop in for a spot of tea or a friendly game of cricket," the Briton growled.

He worked the collective control to gently raise the helicopter and applied pressure to the rudders to steer the craft away from the trees directly above the site below. McCarter pressed the cyclic stick forward a bit and carefully eased in the throttle. The chopper slowed slightly in its flight, barely enough to be noticed by the passengers, let alone by anyone watching from below.

Because they were being watched, all right. In the clearing below, Manning spotted two figures who had their binoculars raised to observe the aircraft. The trees concealed most of the base, and it was impossible to guess how many terrorists were stationed at the site. Manning glimpsed a tent draped in a brown-and-green camouflage net and noticed several armed figures below.

"I see them, too," Calvin James stated, peering from a carriage window with another pair of binoculars. "Looks like our little KGB songbird told us the truth."

"Do you people usually do business this way?" Ricardo Vasquez asked with amazement.

"Anything that works," Katz replied as he used the steel hooks of a trident prosthesis to work the cocking bolt of a Mendoza. "They didn't start shooting, so at least they aren't panicked yet. If we hang around here, they will be. The army claims a convoy was hit by terrorists last night. They'll expect helicopter search parties to start combing the Yucatán. This is a civilian chopper, and they may have even seen it before. Still, they'll get suspicious if we stay in the immediate area."

"We're headed north," McCarter assured him. "I'm not sure I'll be able to find a place to land this bird around here. Bloody jungle doesn't seem to have many bald spots.''

"Keep going about five miles," Katz ordered. "Then lower the chopper to a sturdy tree and we'll get out and climb down to the ground.''

"Who is *we*?" Vasquez asked nervously.

"You're included," Katz informed him. "You will hike back with us to the terrorist base on foot. We'll be in touch with the chopper via radio and let them know when we're close to the base. Then they'll come in to give us air support.''

"You say 'air support' as if it was a squad of fighter jets," Vasquez said. "We're just five men and a helicopter!''

"So it's just a small terrorist base," James said with a shrug. "We're not exactly invading Havana or something.''

"I put together some satchel charges," Manning began as he moved back into the carriage. "Make-shift explosives, and I'm not too sure how powerful the blast will be. If I throw anything out of the chopper when you're down there, don't get too close to them. I'm not sure about the fuses, either. These things might blow in two seconds after they hit the ground, but it might be four or five. If the enemy throws one in your direction, don't assume it's a dud.''

"And you call yourself a demolitions expert," McCarter snorted sourly.

"Shut up and fly," the Canadian replied. "I've got a scope mounted on my M-16, and I'll have a bird's-eye view from the air. Any precision shooting that needs to be done ought to be simple enough unless the pilot crashes this heap."

"I haven't crashed a helicopter in more than a year," McCarter told him. "You blokes better get ready. I'm going to start looking for a tree."

"Right," James said. He turned to Katz. "You figure Rafael is down there, man?"

"I don't know," Katz replied with a sigh. "We'll find out when we get there. I just hope he's still alive."

MAJOR PESCADOR STRUCK a match and held the flame to a cigarette at the corner of his mouth. He puffed smoke from his nostrils as he listened to Captain Raul Encizo explain what had happened to his attack force after the assault on the military truck convoy. Apparently five men had pursued the captain's unit into the jungle. Just five men, but they had been heavily armed and fought well. So well, in fact, that only Captain Encizo and four of the 23rd SCL terrorists survived the confrontation.

It was an embarrassing story. Pescador wished he had taken the captain into his headquarters and listened to the story in private. But he had demanded that the junior officer give him a full report when he'd met the captain's group in the parade field in the middle of the base. The major had been angered by the earlier radio report from the reinforcements sent to assist Captain Encizo's unit. They had encountered the captain, his four remaining men and their prisoner as the group was headed toward the base. The loss of fifteen men outraged Pescador, and he had intended to humiliate the captain by making him explain the high body count in front of the others at the base.

That had been a mistake, Pescador realized too late. The Cuban soldiers and Mexican terrorists had listened with awe as the captain recalled the battle. Captain Encizo's unit had even ambushed the five pursuers, killed one outright and wounded two others, yet the smaller mystery team had managed to wipe out the majority of Encizo's forces. It was not the sort of tale that inspires confidence among the troops.

Pescador had resented Raul Encizo because the other officer was regarded as something of a superman by most of the Cuban soldiers, as well as by the 23rd September Communist League. He was a fearless paratrooper, well versed in the use of small arms, and a martial arts expert who could kill with his bare hands. Now Pescador realized that this superman image had made the captain an inspiration to the others, especially the terrorists who regarded themselves as more powerful than mortal men when armed with a loaded weapon and some explosives.

Nothing had been gained by showing Captain Encizo was just a man, after all.

"So this is the man you took prisoner," Pescador began as he turned to face Rafael Encizo. "Who are you?"

"Does it matter?" Encizo replied bitterly.

He had been force-marched through the jungle with hands bound behind his back. His clothes were torn and his body bruised and sore. Encizo felt worn out, physically and emotionally. His crusade to find his brother had led to nothing except personal disappointment, and death for those who had befriended him in the quest. Encizo had hoped to convince Raul to leave the Cuban army, to return to the United States and become a naturalized citizen as Rafael had. Encizo had even entertained notions about quitting Phoenix Force and starting a small business with his long-lost brother.

"He told Captain Encizo he was his brother," Pedro Garcia announced with amusement. "Maybe you should ask the captain about that."

"I don't recall anyone asking your opinion or even giving you permission to speak, Garcia," Pescador said sharply. He stared at the prisoner. "If you don't talk freely, we'll make you tell us whatever we want to know."

"Torture?" Rafael said with a smile. "I've been through it before. More than once. I was a political prisoner in one of Castro's correctional establishments. Did you know Cuba has at least two hundred political prisons? Why does such a workers' paradise have so much trouble convincing people it is so perfect? Why does such a small island country have need of so many prisons?''

"Just answer my question," Pescador insisted. "Tell me who you are, or let Garcia's friends carve you up like a roast pig."

"He claims his name is Rafael Encizo," Raul declared. "At least, that's what he said when I confronted him. Garcia told you the truth, Comrade Major. This man claims he's my brother."

"*¡Estúpido!*" Pescador spat. "Captain Encizo is an orphan. The state has cared for him since childhood...."

"The same state that murdered our parents," Rafael hissed. "The same Communist dictatorship that sent you here to train terrorists...."

"Shut up!" Pescador snarled, drawing his Makarov. "Open your mouth again, and I'll kill you myself."

"Major," Raul began, a trace of urgency in his voice. "This man might be very valuable to Havana. He's obviously an agent for the CIA or a similar organization."

"Why do you want me to spare his life, Captain?" Pescador demanded. "That doesn't sound like you. You're always eager to kill. You even kill

our own allies during training exercises, Comrade
Captain. Why are you suddenly squeamish?''

"I—I'm thinking of the best interest of the state,"
Raul answered. "If this man is a CIA agent, he's
worth more alive than dead."

"CIA agents don't chase after opponents in the
jungles with no radio contact or backup," Garcia
snickered. "They don't take on four-to-one odds
with automatic weapons, either. Even I know that
much."

"The major told you to shut up, Garcia!" Raul
snapped.

"I want this man executed, whoever he is," Pescador stated. "And I want you to do it, Captain Encizo."

"I am a soldier," Raul said stiffly, "not an exe-
cutioner. I'll kill a man in a fair fight, but cold-
blooded murder is a different matter."

"So kill him your way," Pescador said with a
smile. "We can't give this fellow a weapon, but you
can kill with your hands, Captain. It might be more
interesting that way."

"Comrade Major," Lieutenant Veaga, a Cuban
communications officer began. "I suggest there is no
time for this sort of contest. May I remind you that
a helicopter passed overhead only an hour ago. We
should leave this area quickly as a security precau-
tion."

"This won't take long," Pescador replied. He turned to Raul. "Will it, Captain?"

"Cut the bonds off the prisoner's wrists," Raul replied grimly as he unbuckled his gunbelt. "I want him to be able to defend himself."

A knife blade sliced the ropes at Rafael's wrists. He rubbed his arms to work the circulation back into his limbs. The Cubans and their terrorist allies moved back to form a wide circle around Rafael and Raul. The brothers stood face-to-face, roughly three yards apart. Captain Encizo raised his hands and adopted a fighting stance.

"When we fought each other in Colombia we were interrupted," Raul stated. "This time we fight to the death."

"I don't blame you for any of this, Raul," Rafael told him, rubbing his wrists. "It's not your fault."

Raul shouted a karate *kiai* and charged. He launched a three-pronged attack. Raul snapped a kick for Rafael's groin and thrust a ram's-head punch at his brother's solar plexus while his other hand swung a heel-of-the-palm stroke for Rafael's temple. It was a swift and dangerous attack. Rafael responded automatically. His right thigh blocked the kick. Raul's boot hit hard, and Rafael felt the impact up to his hip. He deflected the punch with a forearm and ducked his head to avoid the other hand.

Rafael almost succeeded. The heel of Raul's hand hit him above the temple. Rafael's head recoiled from the blow, and he staggered backward. The Cuban captain continued his assault and hooked a boot to Rafael's abdomen. The Phoenix Force veteran doubled up from the kick and Raul raised an arm, his hand poised like an ax blade to deliver a lethal stroke to Rafael's neck.

The arm descended. Rafael's arms suddenly rose. His right hand snared Raul's sleeve near the wrist and his left hand grabbed him at the elbow. Rafael turned sharply and dropped to a knee. The captain's forward momentum was abruptly increased, and he hurled head over heels to crash to the ground. Raul had been trained to break his fall, and he shoulder-rolled on impact. He started to rise as Rafael leaped forward. The older Encizo brother hoped to grab Raul from behind and knock him unconscious or apply a sleeper hold to put him out of action without harming him.

Raul caught the movement from the corner of his eye and lashed out a back kick to Rafael's belly. The boot landed hard and expelled the breath from Rafael, driving him backward three feet. Raul whirled and swung a roundhouse kick at his opponent's skull. Rafael ducked, but once again he was not quite quick enough. The boot hit him above the ear. Bright lights of pain exploded inside his skull, and he fell, his head throbbing.

The onlookers cheered when they saw Rafael go down. Raul approached his fallen brother and raised his foot, prepared to stomp Rafael's neck into mush. The Phoenix pro saw the captain through a crimson mist. He lashed out with both feet and slammed into Raul's other leg. The captain was knocked off balance before he could complete the stomp. Raul landed on the ground near his opponent.

Rafael shook his head to clear it and started to rise. The cheers had ceased and there were surprised mutterings that Captain Encizo seemed to be having so much trouble dealing with the prisoner. Raul jumped to his feet and squared off with his opponent. Rafael waited for his brother to attack again. His vision was still slightly blurred, and his left eye fluttered as a welt formed above his ear.

"Kill him, Captain!" Pescador shouted. "Kill him before I decide to have you *both* shot!"

Raul snapped his hands forward in a short, fast motion. Rafael recognized it as a feint. The captain suddenly dropped low and braced himself with one foot and both hands as he swung a leg at Rafael's ankles. The senior Encizo jumped up to avoid the "iron broom" sweep. Raul's leg slashed air and missed its target. He cursed and tried to get to his feet.

Rafael slammed a kick to Raul's chest. The captain grunted and fell to all fours. The Phoenix pro raised his arm and dropped to one knee, then bent his arm and drove a powerful elbow smash into the top of Raul's right shoulder. Bone grated, and Raul gasped in agony as the shoulder popped, dislocated at the joint.

"Sorry," Rafael rasped as he hooked his left fist into his brother's jaw.

Raul's head was jarred by the punch, and he nearly slumped to the ground. Rafael grabbed his hair with one hand and seized Raul's upper left arm with the other. He stood and hauled his brother erect. Rafael whipped his knee up between Raul's splayed legs. The captain groaned in wheezing agony, and his body began to fold at the middle.

Rafael knew he had to finish it one way or the other. He swung a right cross to his brother's face and slashed the side of his left across Raul's right collarbone. The blow caused a fresh wave of pain in the captain's dislocated shoulder. Raul staggered backward, half doubled up and blood oozing from a split lip. His right arm dangled uselessly. Rafael felt his stomach knot, but he did not hesitate. He drove a hard uppercut to his brother's jawbone.

The punch lifted Raul Encizo off his feet and dumped him on the ground in an undignified seated position. The captain glanced up at Rafael, his eyes half-closed and glassy. He tried to get up but landed heavily on his behind. Raul gasped for breath, shook his head and tried to rise once more. He got to his knees but could not find the strength to gain his feet.

"*¡Mierda!*" Garcia spat, looking at Raul as if he was a diseased leper who wanted to marry his sister. "He's finished. Look at him. He can't even get up."

"Not very impressive, Captain," Major Pescador stated with contempt as he stepped forward and pointed his Makarov pistol at Rafael. "Seems I'll have to do this after all."

Rafael Encizo stared at the black muzzle of the gun without blinking. The fear of sudden death was no stranger to the Phoenix Force veteran. He had realized long ago that one day a bullet or a blade would kill him. The time had arrived, and he was determined to face it with dignity.

"No, Major!" Raul declared, his voice slurred by a swollen lip. "I'll do it!"

"*¡Bueno!*" Pescador said with a smile as he held out the pistol for Raul, butt first. "You might redeem yourself after all."

Raul Encizo's left hand gripped the Makarov and took it from Pescador. He propped himself up on one knee and aimed the pistol at Rafael. His finger slowly tightened on the trigger.

17

"¡Adiós, mi hermando!" Raul declared, nodding at Rafael Encizo.

The captain suddenly turned and thrust the pistol into Major Pescador's face. The senior officer's mouth fell open in astonishment a split second before Raul squeezed the trigger. The Makarov roared, and a 9 mm slug punched through Pescador's eyeball, drilling into the socket to destroy the brain.

"¡Madre de—!" Lieutenant Veaga began as he fumbled for his side arm.

Raul Encizo fired and terminated Veaga's cry. The lieutenant's head snapped back with a bullet through the frontal bone. Veaga slumped to the ground next to the corpse of Major Pescador. Raul swung the pistol toward Garcia, but the big terrorist had already trained his AK-47 on the captain's chest.

The Kalashnikov snarled. Two other 23rd SCL terrorists also opened fire. Rafael Encizo screamed in horror and grief as he watched two dozen bullets tear into the torso and face of his younger brother. The force of the high-velocity rounds hurled Captain Encizo two yards backward. His bloodied, mangled corpse landed on the ground near Rafael's feet.

A violent wind suddenly swept across the terrorist camp as if a tornado had descended from the clear blue sky above. A furious sound of huge metal blades slicing air hammered down on them, and the great shadow of a monstrous bird of prey fell across the parade field. The terrorists and remaining Cuban troops glanced up to see the helicopter hover above their base.

David McCarter operated the controls with professional calm while Gary Manning poked the barrel of an M-16 out the open door of the carriage. The Canadian triggered the weapon expertly and fired 3-round bursts. A terrorist received a trio of 5.56 mm slugs through the heart. A Cuban sergeant started to raise his rifle, but Manning nailed him in the face and forehead with another burst of his M-16. Another terrorist fired a hasty volley of Kalashnikov ammo at the chopper. Bullets raked the metal frame of the aircraft.

"Not even close," Manning muttered as he took out the gunman with three well-placed rounds to the chest.

McCarter raised the whirlybird into the sky as the survivors fired upward or scrambled for safety. Four men on the ground ran straight into the path of 9 mm rounds as Yakov Katzenelenbogen appeared at the edge of the camp with his Mendoza braced across his prosthetic arm. The enemy went down after a brief frenzy of dancing.

Several terrorists rushed into a tent where Russian RPG rocket launchers were stored. Manning took the opportunity to take out a whole group and dropped a satchel from the copter. It landed on the canvas roof of the tent just as a terrorist emerged with a launcher braced across his shoulder. He raised it to aim it at the helicopter.

The satchel charge exploded. The blast detonated rockets stored inside the tent. The second explosion sent a tremor through the camp like a minor earthquake. The tent was gone. Only some burning fragments remained, along with the spewed-out remnants of what had been human bodies.

Pedro Garcia and another terrorist headed for the jungle to the east of the base. Calvin James was ready for them. The black hard guy from Chicago fired an M-16 and drilled three holes in the chest of Carcia's comrade. The flunky cried out and fell as Garcia tried to locate his new opponent.

"Here you go," James rasped, and fired a 3-round burst into Garcia's stomach.

The big terrorist howled and dropped his AK-47. He fell to his knees, hugging his bleeding abdomen and quivering in pain. James jogged forward and lashed a hard kick to Garcia's face. The terrorist flopped onto his back, unconscious and rapidly dying. James had no more time for Garcia as he sought out more opponents and opened fire.

The 23rd SCL fanatics found death at every turn. Another satchel charge blasted the largest tent in the compound, taking out the barracks section. Katz ducked behind the cover of a thick gum tree and continued to cut down opponents with his Mendoza. James and Vasquez trapped the enemy in a cross fire with their M-16s. The terrorists had no cover and nowhere to run.

The last two Cuban soldiers among the group ran to the shed that served as Pescador's headquarters. One of them slipped inside, perhaps to send a radio message. The other stood near the door and yanked the pin from a F-1 fragmentation grenade. He raised his fist and prepared to hurl the grenade at Katz's position.

Rafael Encizo saw the Cuban soldier who was about to throw the frag. He scooped up the Makarov next to Raul's body and fired three rounds as fast as he could squeeze off the shots. Encizo's aim was blurred by hot tears in his eyes, but two rounds slammed into the soldier's upper chest. The impact spun him around, and the grenade fell from his grasp to land inside the headquarters shack. The frag exploded, and the flimsy building flew apart like a house of cards. The wreckage caved in on the mutilated bodies of the two Havana-bred troopers.

A wounded terrorist crawled to the corpse of a comrade and braced his Kalashnikov across the lifeless form to use it as a benchrest. One of his arms had been crushed by shrapnel from an explosion. He placed the butt to his shoulder and slipped the index finger of his good hand inside the trigger guard. The fanatic smiled as he pointed the rifle at Rafael Encizo's back. The son of a bitch was responsible for this carnage, and he figured his last act on earth might as well be one of revenge.

Three M-16 bullets suddenly descended from the sky and split open the top of his head. Brains and blood spilled from his shattered skull, and he expired before he could squeeze the trigger.

Up above, Gary Manning raised his rifle as he peered down from the carriage door of the helicopter. "I think that's the last of them, David!" the Canadian shouted to McCarter.

"We'll make another pass just to make sure," the Briton replied. "You might get that rope ladder ready in case the fighting is over so our mates can climb up and join us. Be a long walk out of here."

"I can't argue with you on that," Manning agreed.

As the shadow of the whirlybird swung away from the base, Katz signaled to James and Vasquez to hold their fire. There was no one left to shoot. The Cuban military personnel and the terrorists had been slaughtered by the ruthless Phoenix Force assault. Katz slowly approached Rafael Encizo. The Cuban member of the special commando team sat on the ground with the blood-streaked head of Captain Raul Encizo held to his chest.

"Rafael," Katz said in a firm yet gentle voice. "It's over, Rafael. We have to leave now."

"Katz?" Encizo replied, uncertain if the Israeli was a mirage or a distortion in his clouded vision. "How did you find me?"

"We'll explain later, man," James assured him. "Half the Mexican army is gonna be poking around here in a couple hours, and we don't want to be here when they show up."

"Yeah," Encizo said with a nod. Tears rolled down his cheeks as he cradled Raul's head in his arms. "I found my brother. Guess I'll have to leave him...again."

"Oh, Jesus," Calvin James whispered. "We gotta get outta here, Rafael."

Encizo nodded again. He kissed Raul's cold, lifeless brow and gently lowered him to the ground. Reluctantly he rose to his feet and waited for the helicopter to return.

All around, the jungle swelled with the sounds of life, in sharp contrast to death's recent visit to the clearing. Encizo glanced at his companions, then looked away. He felt numb and oblivious to the bright sunlight and riot of color. The only thing that drummed inside his head was the knowledge that Raul was dead.

But one more thing did get through to him. As Katz faced him and put his hand on the Cuban's shoulder, he said, "You've done your best, Rafael. You've gone to the very end."

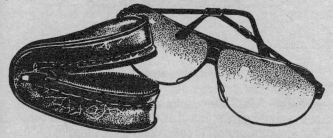

Phoenix Force—bonded in secrecy to avenge the acts of terrorists everywhere.

Super Phoenix Force #2

American ''killer'' mercenaries are involved in a KGB plot to overthrow the government of a South Pacific island. The American President, anxious to preserve his country's image and not disturb the precarious position of the island nation's government, sends in the experts—Phoenix Force—to prevent a coup.